# POLICE AND THIEVES

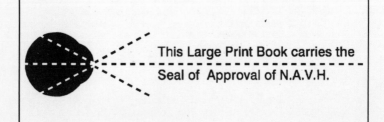

This Large Print Book carries the
Seal of Approval of N.A.V.H.

BRIDGER

# POLICE AND THIEVES

## JAMES PATRICK HUNT

**THORNDIKE PRESS**
*A part of Gale, Cengage Learning*

GALE
CENGAGE Learning™

Detroit • New York • San Francisco • New Haven, Conn • Waterville, Maine • London

GALE
CENGAGE Learning™

LIBRARY OF CONGRESS CATALOGING-IN-PUBLICATION DATA

Hunt, James Patrick, 1964–
Police and thieves : Bridger / by James Patrick Hunt.
    p. cm. — (Thorndike Press large print mystery)
ISBN-13: 978-1-4104-4291-8 (hardcover)
ISBN-10: 1-4104-4291-8 (hardcover)
    1. Thieves—Fiction. 2. Murder—Investigation—Fiction. 3. Seattle (Wash.)—Fiction. 4. Large type books. I. Title.
PS3608.U577P65 2011b
813'.6—dc22                                                        2011032335

Published in 2011 by arrangement with Tekno Books and Ed Gorman.

Printed in the United States of America
1 2 3 4 5 6 7 15 14 13 12 11

# POLICE AND THIEVES

# ONE

The parole officer parked his car outside the apartment building. He locked the car and walked to the unit where he would meet his client. The unit was in an apartment complex that was considered low-income housing. Most of the inhabitants were black. The parole officer was white. The tenants knew the parole officer was the law because he drove an ugly, unmarked state car with a dull paint job and a barebones interior. The parole officer was armed. He had a .38 snub-nose Chief's Special and a pair of handcuffs. But to the tenants who knew him, he was more of a social worker than a cop. Many cops shared this view of probation and parole officers.

The parole officer walked up three flights of stairs and knocked on a door.

"Who is it?"

"It's Seth."

A pause. "Is it Wednesday?"

"Yeah, it's Wednesday. Are you dressed, Natoya?"

"Yeah, I'm dressed."

"Let me in then."

The parole officer's voice was firm but polite. He had many of the powers given to law enforcement officers, but he did not abuse them. He took pride in having never mistreated one of his clients.

Natoya Carter opened the door. She was dressed in knee-length shorts and a T-shirt. Twenty-four years old, she was black, heavy and poor. A few months ago, she had sold a quarter gram of crack to an undercover Seattle cop. The deal was recorded on video. She was arrested and assigned a public defender. A week later, in the judge's chambers, the public defender argued entrapment to the judge, but the judge said he'd seen the videotape and it didn't look like entrapment to him. The public defender said he respected the judge's view, but there was a possibility that a jury would disagree. The assistant prosecutor let out one of his practiced sighs of weary disgust and the judge smiled and said, sure, that was possible. The public defender turned to the prosecutor and asked him what good it would do to put another penny ante dope dealer in prison. The prosecutor said it was his job to punish, not to help, and the public defender asked him if he was running for office. The judge told them both to knock it off and asked them if it was true that Natoya Carter had a baby. The public defender said yes, that was true, and hoped for the best. The judge then asked the prosecutor if he would agree to a two-year sentence, suspended, with six months' probation under the usual rules and conditions. The prosecutor went along with it and Natoya Carter was added to the probation and parole officer's roster.

Now the parole officer stepped into her apartment.

Natoya said, "Hi, Seth."

"Hello, Natoya. How are you?"

"I'm good. You need me to . . . ?"

She was asking him if he wanted her to go to the bathroom and pee in a little plastic cup so he could take it back to a lab and have it tested for traces of illegal narcotics. Under her rules and conditions of probation, he could request it.

Seth said, "No, that's all right. Just let me look at your arms."

She sat at the kitchen table and turned her arms over so the parole officer could examine her wrists and the undersides of her elbows. He saw no tracks. The parole officer also looked at her face and eyes. They seemed okay and he did not smell the telltale atrocious odor that is often present with meth or coke users. Natoya cooperated with him and did not give him any attitude or hostile body language. She liked her parole officer. He had never dissed her or treated her like she was a piece of shit like a lot of other cops she had dealt with.

The parole officer said, "How's the job search going?"

"Okay," she said, and he knew he was going to get a story. He had gotten used to the excuses and explanations of his clients. He did not take the embellishments or fabrications personally. "I talked with the assistant manager at that deli I told you about?"

"Yes?"

"I talked with her and she said they may not be able to hire me because of Colby?"

"Your son?"

"Yeah."

"The assistant manager asked you if you had a child?"

"Yeah."

"Well, they're not supposed to do that."

"They not?"

"No, they're not."

"Why not?"

"Because it's the law. Potential employers are not supposed to ask you if you have children."

"That's the law? Oh yeah, you going to law school, right?"

"Right."

"How you do that and do this?"

"I'm going at night. Part time. Listen, Natoya, I told you before, I can't help you if you're not straight with me. Did they really ask you if you had a baby or did you tell them that on your own?"

"Well . . . I may have told them. Was that okay?"

"It depends. If you told them that because you didn't want them to hire you, I don't think that'd be too cool. After all, your mother's taking care of Colby."

"Mostly."

"If you don't have a job, there's a greater chance you'll drift back to hanging around with the wrong people. And you do that you'll end up in trouble with the law and then the prosecutor will want to revoke your probation and put you in jail. I don't want that, your mother doesn't want that, your son doesn't want that and you don't want that. Okay?"

"Okay."

"Keep working on it, Natoya. Will you do

that for me?"

"I will, Seth."

"And we'll talk about it some more next week."

The parole officer did a cursory search of the apartment to check for drugs or weapons or signs of a boyfriend. He didn't see any and was glad of it. If he had found drugs or weapons he would have to arrest her. He would not have enjoyed doing that, but he would have done it.

The parole officer left the apartment and walked down the stairs.

A light rain was coming down. It would clear off by lunch and the sun would come out and it might be a pretty afternoon, but the rain would come back in the evening as it always did in this city. It had taken him a few years to get used to the Seattle climate. Now he believed he liked it.

The parole officer checked his watch. Not quite 9:30. He would stop for a cup of coffee and write down some notes on Carter, Natoya, Case No. 09-512. If he moved quickly and saw no violations, he should be able to get in four more home visits before lunch.

He reached his car and put the key in the lock and heard a voice say, "Hey, man." He turned to see a guy wearing a dark blue knit

12

cap pulled over his ears. The man held a long-barreled .22 pistol. The parole officer drew breath and started to say something, but the man brought the pistol up and shot the parole officer in the forehead. Then shot him again. The parole officer fell to the ground and the killer bent over him and shot him two more times, even though the parole officer was already dead.

# TWO

Bridger followed the group of lawyers as they left their offices and walked to a restaurant for lunch. It was a hot, humid March afternoon, more like summer than spring, which was how it usually was in Houston. The lawyers took a four-top table in a Jewish deli and took their coats off and set them on the backs of their chairs. They all wore expensive white starched shirts and none of them rolled their sleeves up. Young fellows with good haircuts and Hugo Boss ties. A pretty girl of about nineteen brought them their menus and a couple of them gave her big smiles and Bridger saw then how he could do it.

He took a seat nearby and ordered a chicken salad sandwich on toast, no mayo, and a cup of coffee. The lawyers talked about the cases they were second chairing and a little about cars and homes and then they smiled some more at the cute waitress when she brought them their check. They stood to leave and Bridger walked by their table, nudging into one as he put on his jacket. Bridger mumbled a pardon and the lawyer mumbled one back. The lawyers left and Bridger went to the restroom and into a stall and when he got there he pulled the lawyer's wallet out of his jacket pocket.

Inside he found the magnetic card that would get him into the law offices.

It was between two and three A.M. when he came to the office building. It didn't look formidable and it wasn't formidable. A seven-story office building in suburban Houston that had been built during the oil-rich seventies. The oil bust tore through the town and left the building at a third occupancy and that was in a good year. The law firm of Davies and Berry bought the building in full a few years later, getting it at a bargain price. The firm employed approximately two hundred lawyers and a staff of another two hundred. They used all of the building.

It was white and more hexagonal than rectangular, with dark tinted windows that couldn't be opened, and an atrium going from the bottom to the top. Each floor above the first had a balcony where you could peer down and look where there used to be a fountain. A seventies design that was dated now. There was a parking garage at the bottom, the garage doors at the back of the building.

Bridger had staked out the place before. He knew that at this hour there would be one security guard. The one he had seen before had been a fat man in his sixties wearing a light blue uniform and a six-shooter at his side. Probably a retired police officer. There was no desk at the entrance to the building, but there was a small room on the first floor that was more of a break room than an office. It was a law firm, not a bank. But they had taken some precautions. The security guard would have no way of knowing what was kept inside.

Bridger had left his car at a restaurant two miles away. He had walked here. He was dressed in a dark suit and a white shirt and he wore black shoes with rubber soles. He carried an attaché case. In the case he had his tools, including a .45 pistol.

Bridger was a big man of about forty, with the appearance of a former professional athlete who had kept fit after retirement. His hair was cut short and was graying at the temples. In his suit, he could pass for a lawyer himself or a mid-level sales executive.

Now he walked among the cars in the parking lot. He stayed in the shadows and through the windows he saw the security guard. Only it was a different guy than the one he'd seen before. This one was younger, maybe around thirty. He wore a blond crewcut and he had an automatic pistol holstered at his waist. Probably a Glock .40. Younger and in better shape than the fat man he'd seen a few weeks ago. Probably meaner too.

It made him uneasy. It was unexpected. But then he told himself, well . . . so what? There was still just one of him.

Bridger watched the security guard walk the perimeter of the first floor. Then he saw the security guard get into the elevator.

Bridger went up to the side door then, holding his magnetic key to the door. The light went from red to green and Bridger pushed the door and walked in. He walked to the elevators. There were two of them. The sign between the elevators listed all the lawyers in the firm, the partners at the top left. He looked at the light above the elevator and saw that the car stopped on the fifth floor. The office Bridger was going to was on the seventh. Bridger took the stairs to the seventh.

He kept his steps quiet. He reached the seventh floor and went to the front door of the law offices. The door was locked. From his pocket he removed two thin steel door picks, using one at the top and another at the bottom. He felt these out and removed a set of skeleton keys from his pocket. He had seven of them. He picked out the sixth and inserted it into the lock. He tried to turn it but it wouldn't go. He went to the seventh key but that didn't work either. He went back to the sixth and worked on it with a small thin file, getting the configuration he needed. After that he put the skeleton back in and the lock turned. He let himself in. He made sure he locked the door behind him.

There was a red leather couch in the reception area and two matching red leather chairs. Behind the reception area, there was a small kitchen area. There were six offices in this suite. The one he was looking for belonged to a lawyer named Bill Atkinson. Atkinson was in the middle of a long, drawn-out divorce and his wife had claimed that he was hiding assets from her. These assets included approximately $185,000 worth of diamonds. Marital property, maybe, but Bridger had received a tip that

Atkinson was keeping them in a safe in his office. Now Bridger was in the suite, but there were no names on the office doors indicating whose office was whose. He went through the offices with his penlight, playing its small beam over the walls and desks. In the fourth office, he saw William Atkinson's law degree on the wall. Bridger closed the door to this office. The desk was locked. Bridger set his attaché case on the desk and opened it and took out an ice pick. He used the ice pick to break the lock in the desk drawer. But he found nothing when he went through the drawers.

He searched the cabinets behind the desk. In one of the cabinets he found a thick set of Martindale-Hubbell books. He was no lawyer, but he sensed that such books were more for display than use so he pulled the books out and then he found the safe.

More than once he had found safes that were not locked. People could be funny about that sort of thing. Buy a safe to feel important, then quit locking it because it was a pain in the ass. He pulled the handle on the safe to see if it would open, but it didn't. Locked.

Bridger pulled out a piece of two-sided sticky tape. He placed the tape a few inches to the side of the lock. The strip went from the top of the safe door to the bottom. Then he removed the cover to the tape so that it too was sticky. Then he took a small cube of C-4 plastic explosive and applied it to the sticky tape strip. Into one end of the C-4 strip he inserted a detonator. There were two wires coming out of the detonator. Bridger made sure they were separated. Then he attached them to an electric cord. He took a large plastic kitchen bag out of the case and walked to the kitchen area. In the kitchen he filled the bag with water. He carried the bag back to the office and hung the yellow loops over a cabinet doorknob. Now the weight of the water-filled bag rested against the safe. He studied it for a moment. Then he walked back to the reception area and took the two large cushions off the leather couch and rested them against the water-filled bag. He moved one of the office chairs to the other side of the office and positioned it in front of the wall socket. Then he crouched down behind the chair and stuck the plug in the socket.

The explosion was not much louder than that of a car exhaust backfiring. It echoed off the walls of the office but hopefully didn't sound beyond the suite. Bridger came out from behind the chair. Water gushed from the punctured bag onto the carpet. The sofa cushions had been thrown back against the desk. The desk itself was not damaged.

Bridger cleared away the bag. A nice, neat incision was now in the safe door. Bridger opened the newly fashioned door and reached inside. He found the bag with the diamonds and took a quick look at them. He put them in his jacket pocket. Then he put all his tools back in the attaché case.

He walked out of the office suite, making sure the door was locked behind him, then he walked to the stairwell and started down. He kept going until he reached the lowest level, which was the entrance to the underground parking garage. There were only three vehicles down there. A Ford pick-up, a Mercedes convertible and a Lincoln Navigator. All three of the vehicles had been there before when he had cased the building. He knew that the Lincoln had a remote inside that would open the electric garage door. He was walking to the Lincoln when the elevator door dinged and out stepped the security guard.

Bridger stopped and turned. He looked at the security guard and the security guard looked back at him.

*You're a lawyer,* Bridger thought. *A lawyer wearing a dark suit and a tie. That's what you are and that's what he sees.*

Bridger said, "How are you doing?"

"Good," the guard said. "Working late tonight?"

"Yeah. Got an early appearance in court tomorrow. Had to pick some things up."

The security guard held his hands at his side in a way Bridger didn't like. He was not a tall man, but he was thick and heavy in the chest and shoulders. Bridger wondered if the guy took steroids.

The guard said, "I thought I heard some noise upstairs. Like a chair being knocked over or something. Did you hear anything?"

Bridger shrugged. "No. But I'm so damn tired. You know how that is." Bridger gave him an easy, non-threatening smile.

The guard did not smile back and then his eyes dropped to Bridger's hands. And Bridger knew what he was looking at.

The guard said, "How come you're wearing gloves?"

"What?"

"It's almost eighty degrees outside. Why are you wearing gloves?"

Bridger started to say, "I've got a medical problem —"

But the guard had pulled his gun on him, holding it now with two hands as he trained it on Bridger.

The guard said, "Put the case down and put your hands on your head."

"Wait a minute. I —"

*"Put the case down and put your hands on your head. Now."*

"Sir. Do you know what you're doing? I *work* here."

The security guard came toward him, holding his gun steady. Bridger set the case on the ground and held his hands in front of him. He could read this guy, could read that the guard was looking for a reason to shoot him. The guard got near and ordered Bridger to turn around.

"All right, all right," Bridger sounding angry but scared too, as a white-bread lawyer would sound. He put his hands on his head and turned around and he heard the guard reach for a pair of handcuffs and that was when Bridger made a sharp twist, putting his body into it, and slammed his elbow into the guard's face. The guard cried out and Bridger turned on him and put one hand on the gun and used the other to chop the guard in the neck. Bridger twisted the gun out of his hand. The gun clattered to the ground and the guard reached for it. Bridger kicked the gun away. The guard rushed him, grappling him. Bridger held onto him and brought his knee up into the guard's face. He did it two more times and the guard slumped to the ground.

Bridger ran back to his case and picked it up. Then he quickly got into the Lincoln Navigator. It took him a minute or so to get it started. Once or twice he looked over to see the guard and make sure the guy was still on the ground, hopefully unconscious. Bridger got the Lincoln engine going and he looked once more. The guard was on his knees now, looking at him, then looking to his left.

Where Bridger had kicked the gun.

The guard ran to the gun and Bridger put the Lincoln in gear.

The guard reached the gun and started firing shots into the Lincoln as Bridger accelerated it to the door, pushing the pedal to the floor, not bothering to look for the automatic door opener. Two shots cracked into the rear window then the Lincoln smashed through the garage door and into the night.

He ditched the Lincoln in a crowded parking lot about a mile away. He hurried to a bus stop. He put his gloves in the attaché case and put on a pair of reading glasses and started working on a crossword puzzle. His heart beat anxiously as nine minutes passed before the bus came. He boarded the bus and he felt better. The bus route took him past the office building he had broken into. There were no police cars there yet. But when they passed it he saw a patrol unit hurry by, its lights flashing. He stayed on the bus as it went downtown. He got off there and walked to a Sheraton hotel where he hailed a cab. He took the cab back to the parking lot where he had left his car.

He dumped the clothes in a trash can fifty miles outside of the city. By sunrise he was in Mississippi.

# THREE

He stayed the night in a small hotel near Atlanta. He slept with the .45 next to his bed. Not because he feared the police would find him there. It was to protect himself against anyone breaking and entering into his hotel room. He always stayed at cheap, small hotels in cheap, small towns. He always paid cash and if he was on a job, he never signed his real name to a register.

Dan Bridger had been to jail once. That was in Indiana, the state where he was born. He learned a few things about himself there. One of these things was his true nature. Another was that most criminals were dumbasses unwilling to step outside themselves and ask themselves what they did wrong. Not morally wrong, but stupid wrong. He heard guys talk in prison as if they had wanted to get caught. Maybe they did. Most all of them said the system fucked them, never that they had fucked themselves. In Bridger's view, they were unprofessional. He had studied his craft in prison and developed a few rules and usually he stuck with them. A couple of years ago, he had broken one of his rules and as a result had gone through a week of some highly unpleasant shit with some Philadelphia mobsters. He had been set up and framed, but when he looked back on it he still mostly blamed himself for being dumb.

He lay in his motel bed in Georgia and thought about Houston. If the security guard had not seen his gloves, he would have walked out of there easy. Bad luck or had he been stupid? One of his rules was always wear gloves. He had a criminal record and his prints were in the national AFIS system. He could not leave fingerprints. So . . . what should he have done? Taken off the gloves before he stole the car in case he ran into a cop or a guard. But if he had done that he might have left prints on the vehicle, no matter how careful he would have been to wipe it down, and that could have been traced back to him.

Well, it was done. He had escaped with over a hundred thousand dollars' worth of diamonds. He had had to rough up the security guard, but he hadn't killed him. The security guard would be all right.

Besides, the security guard had wanted to kill him. Of that he had no doubt.

He slept nine hours. In the morning he showered, dressed and left the room. He drove his work car — a Buick Park Avenue — to a convenience store to get breakfast. He ate in the car. Twelve hours later he was in Baltimore, Maryland, where he lived.

He drove the Buick to a small garage he owned that was near the Dundalk Marine Terminals. The garage was one of his secrets. It was not registered in his name. He unlocked the garage and drove the Buick in. He removed the Texas plates from the Buick. Then he stored the plates and his attaché case and its tools behind a secret wall. Then he got into a blue '74 Chevy Nova and drove it out of the garage. He left it running when he manually locked the garage. He got back in the Nova and drove to his house.

He lived in the Rodgers Forge neighborhood north of the city. He owned a modest row house with a red brick front that had ivy and shrubs covering most of it and a small stone porch that was well shaded. There was a small path leading up to the house, three stone steps that had crumbled and become crooked over the years. Bridger had left it alone. He lived alone and he had

28

very few visitors.

The house had three floors, not counting the basement. A dining room and a living room and a kitchen on the first floor, three bedrooms and a bathroom on the second. He never used the attic and it had become musty and hot.

He had owned the house for several years. He had grown tired of it in the last year, however, and he wasn't sure why. He had lost a close friend, a woman, and he wondered if that had had something to do with it. Maybe it did. Or maybe it was the fact that a lot of young families had moved into the neighborhood and most of the older neighbors had died. The young husbands would question him about football or work or the latest news and he wasn't good at that sort of thing. He didn't like having to hide in the house all the time.

He drove the Nova through the back alley and parked in the garage behind his house. He watched a little news. Then he went upstairs and went to bed.

The woman was telling Alan Monfort that she didn't need six chairs, just four. Monfort said, "Mrs. Kepel, I don't think you understand. I can't sell you four. You have to buy all six."

"But it won't work with six. Have you seen my dining room? The symmetry will be all messed up. Sophie says."

"I know what Sophie says. I know she's your interior decorator and she's your dear, dear friend. But I know this set better than she does. If you want a set of four chairs, I can show you something else. But I won't split this set up."

They were discussing six chairs Monfort had bought in Maine. Six New England Hepplewhite dining chairs in superb untouched condition. They had retained their original finish, leather seats and brass tacks. They were descended from the family of the Royal Governor of Portsmouth, John Wentworth. Monfort was not shining the lady to get extra money out of her. The notion of separating four chairs from the six genuinely offended his aesthetic sensibility.

Mrs. Kepel said, "Would you mind discussing this with Sophie?"

"Yes," Monfort said. "Excuse me."

He motioned Bridger back to his office. Bridger closed the door.

Monfort said, "How are you, Danny?"

"Good." Bridger handed him the bag.

Monfort poured the diamonds on his desk. He pulled his diamond gauge and jeweler's eye out of his desk drawer.

Alan Monfort owned a tony antique store in Pikesville. His customers were mainly wealthy women. He was in his late fifties and reminded Bridger a little bit of Tony Randall. He was fussy and neat and he took his antiques very seriously. He would not sell his wares to people he did not believe were sufficiently appreciative. There were some pieces he kept in the front room, but refused to sell. Bridger once asked him why he displayed them if he wasn't willing to sell them. Alan said Bridger wouldn't understand. Alan was the best fence Bridger had ever worked with.

Now he said, "Yes, yes, yes. Nice cuts. Very nice work. Yes . . . well, I'll need a little more time to examine these, but I think I can get you about sixty-five, maybe seventy for these."

"By when?"

"Next week."

"That'll work."

"Oh. Are you interested in another job?"

"You mean —"

"No, I mean a restoration job. A fellow I know bought an old Austin Healey, '61 I believe. Could you handle that?"

"Maybe. It would cost him less to buy a new car, though."

"It always does. I'll have him call you."

■ ■ ■ ■

Bridger drove to the mechanic's garage near Hampden. It was a different garage from the one he kept near the waterfront. There was a faded red and white sign that said *A&T Automotive Repair.* There were three cars parked on the side, one American, the others foreign.

Bridger's partner at the auto repair shop was Sonny Ma. Sonny had come from Vietnam in 1975, one of the boat people. He was a good mechanic. Now he was smoking a cigarette, taking a break.

Bridger said hello to him. Sonny nodded back. Bridger passed him to go to the back office where he would change into coveralls.

Sonny said, "You got a message. I left it on the desk."

"About a car?"

"No. She said it was personal."

"Who was it?"

"It's on your desk."

He saw the name with a number beneath it. He called the number. A woman answered.

"Elaine Ogilvie?"

"This is Elaine."

"This is Dan Bridger, A&T Automotive. I

had a message you called."

A pause. Then a different voice. "Daniel Bridger?"

"Yes."

"Daniel Bridger, Baltimore, Maryland?"

"Yes. What do you want?"

"You have a brother named Seth?"

Now Bridger paused. "Yes."

"I'm sorry to tell you this, but your brother's dead."

# FOUR

The plane touched down at the Seattle airport. Bridger pulled his carry-on bag from the upper compartment and walked off behind the others. He rented a Lincoln Continental and drove to the girl's apartment.

When he had got off the phone at his shop in Baltimore, Sonny must have looked at him and saw something was wrong. Bridger told him he was going to have to leave town for a few days. Sonny never asked where Bridger was going when he left town — he knew better — but this time he said, "Is everything okay?"

Bridger said, "My brother died."

Sonny said he was sorry. Then, a moment later, he said, "I didn't know you had a brother."

Elaine Ogilvie's apartment was on the second floor of a house that looked more house than duplex. The house sat across the street from an elementary school. It was the morning recess and children were running around on the playground. It was cool and wet and the skies were gray and most of the kids wore jackets and rain boots.

There were two doors on the front porch of the house, one of them for the apartment on the first floor, the other in front of a flight of stairs going up to the second floor. Bridger rang the bell on the door in front of the stairs. Rang it again and heard a woman's voice on the intercom.

"Who is it?"

"Dan Bridger."

There was a buzz and the door lock released. Bridger went in, closing the door behind him. He stood at the bottom of the steps and looked up to see a young woman looking down at him.

She seemed almost plain at first glance. Short straight hair that was more brown than blond. A straight line of a mouth, glasses covering her eyes. She wore jeans and an oversized brown sweater.

Bridger said, "Are you Elaine?"

"Yes. You're Dan."

"Yeah. Do you mind talking to me?"

"Why would I mind?" she said, her tone curt, almost bitter.

Bridger didn't say anything.

The girl said, "Come on up. I've made some coffee."

They sat on opposite sides of a small red table in the kitchen. The kitchen was modestly outfitted — an old-fashioned white gas stove with a pipe going up to the ceiling and cheap, ugly linoleum on the floor. The refrigerator was old and green and there was a photo held up there with a magnet. Seth Bridger and the girl laughing and smiling at a casino in Vegas, a monkey between them.

Bridger said, "Did he live here with you?"

"Yes."

"How did you know him?"

"We met in law school. In evidence class. He was . . ."

"Yes?"

"Different. He was a gentleman. I'm a full-time student, he was part time. He had a job, you know, he worked days as a probation and parole officer."

"A probation and parole officer?"

"Yes."

"How long had he been doing that?"

"Five years." The girl looked at him. "Didn't you know?"

"No."

"When was the last time you saw him?"

"Eight years ago."

"Eight years ago . . . that was when his mother died. You saw him at her funeral?"

"Yeah."

"And not since."

"No."

Elaine Ogilvie looked at him, her expression curious, but a little hard too. She said, "Was there a problem between you two?"

"I don't think so. We just weren't close. There was no fight, no falling-out." Bridger shrugged.

The girl seemed to steady herself, as if to avoid physically recoiling.

Bridger felt the need to say, "I'm grateful to you. For calling me."

"Are you?"

Bridger sighed. "Look," he said, "my brother is — was — ten years younger than me. I left home when I was seventeen, joined the Navy. He was seven. We didn't keep in touch."

"You mean *you* didn't."

"Neither one of us." Bridger sighed again and made some sort of gesture that didn't help. He didn't know what he was supposed to do about it now.

Elaine said, "He told me your family life — yours and his — wasn't very happy."

"It wasn't."

37

"That your dad drank."

"Yeah."

"And sometimes beat you."

"Sometimes."

"You more than Seth?"

"Yeah. Until I got big enough to hit back. He stopped then."

"He also told me that your mother didn't do anything to stop him. That she was indifferent to the pain he inflicted on her children."

"That's about right."

"And you left a seven-year-old with that."

For a while Bridger didn't look at her. Then he said, "Yeah, I guess I did. Did he tell you that too?"

"No. He said he would've done the same thing in your place. He said you got it worse than he did. He said you were bigger than him, stronger and meaner. He said when he was young he wished he was like you."

"Did he?"

"Yes. But he didn't grow up to be big or mean. He was about half a foot shorter than you. He was strong, though. In the right ways. Strong, but gentle."

"I'm sorry for your loss."

"Does it show?"

"Yeah. Were you . . . did you have plans?"

"Plans, you mean to marry?"

38

"Yes."

"Yeah. We talked about it. We wanted to wait until we both finished school. But things don't — yes, we were very tight." The girl stopped to steady herself. Bridger could see the streaks on her face where she had cried before.

"I'm sorry," Bridger said again.

"You're sorry," she said. "You're sorry for my loss. What about you? Aren't you sorry for *your* loss? He was your brother."

Bridger said nothing.

"I mean, don't you feel anything?"

Bridger asked, "How did you know where to reach me?"

"Seth told me about you. What little he knew. He said you were a mechanic in Baltimore."

"Did he say anything else?"

"He said when he was little, when he was little, sometimes you would take him fishing with you. He said you would just pick him up and say, 'I'm taking him with me.' And carry him out the door. He said that when you did that, he knew he was safe. He said that you didn't talk to him much, but that you would watch over him so that he wouldn't wander off or fall in the water. He said you never talked much, with anyone in the family."

Bridger was quiet.

And the girl said, "And he also told me that you went to prison for grand larceny. And that he thinks you're probably still a professional criminal."

"He said that?"

"Yeah." The girl looked at him again and said, "If he was right about that, maybe it was good that you stayed away from him."

"Maybe it was." Bridger said, "What happened?"

"He was visiting an offender. He called them clients. He was visiting a client at an apartment complex called Wood Creek. It's a rough place. A lot of . . . poor people."

"You mean blacks?"

"That's not what I meant."

Bridger thought it was, but didn't really care. "Go on," he said.

"There's a lot of gang activity there. In any low-income housing, you'll find that. The police said he left there after visiting his client and someone came up and shot him in the head. Took his wallet and left."

"Was he armed?"

"Armed?"

"Did he carry a gun? I mean for work?"

"Yes. He was a sort of social worker, but by state law, he was a peace officer too. Yes, he carried a gun."

"Did the shooter take that too?"

"No. In fact, the detective called me today. The police detective called and told me I could come get it."

"Have you gotten it?"

"No. I don't want it. I hate guns. I don't think Seth much liked them either."

"He carried one."

"Because he was supposed to. He didn't like it."

"Did he like being a probation and parole officer?"

"I don't think so. He thought about applying to Seattle PD, but he would have to wait two years to get into the academy. So he got a job as a parole officer. He started out liking it, but he said it got pretty depressing."

"Why was that?"

"He said it became too familiar. That nothing ever changed. He worked with people who became parole officers because they couldn't become cops. Too fat or too lazy. Most of the people he worked with hated their clients. They looked for ways to revoke their probation. They enjoyed arresting them and sending them to prison. But Seth wasn't like that. He wanted them to go straight, to get better."

"Most of them don't want to go straight."

41

The girl frowned. "You sound like some of his co-workers."

"Sorry."

"Anyway, he wasn't self-pitying or anything. He had just lost faith in what he was doing. He realized he wasn't changing anything. He didn't like most of the people he worked with and he didn't like putting people in jail."

"He was going to quit?"

"When he finished law school, yes."

"Do you know the name of the person he was visiting before he was killed?"

"I don't."

"Did the police suspect he or she had anything to do with it?"

"I don't think so."

"What did the police tell you?"

"They're still investigating it. But a uniformed officer told me it was probably just a gangbanger robbing him. That he was in the wrong place at the wrong time."

"What do you think?"

"What do *I* think?"

"Yeah."

"Two years ago, I was a college student at Washington State, going to fraternity parties, smoking dope and listening to music. I'm twenty-four years old. I haven't . . . experienced anything. I'm just a student.

This is beyond my ken."

"So you believe the police?"

"What should I do?"

Bridger didn't answer her. He asked, "Where is he now? His body."

"At the downtown morgue. I haven't — we haven't scheduled a funeral. Funny as it may seem, you were his only family."

"How involved were you?"

"Very."

"Maybe we can arrange something. I'll pay for it."

The girl snorted, letting him know the offer wasn't well taken. She said, "I'm not asking you for anything. I want to make that *very* clear. I called you for him, that's it."

"I got it. Where are your parents?"

"They're in Spokane."

"Why don't you go stay with them for a couple of days?"

"Why? You don't think I should be alone?"

"I didn't say that."

Elaine Ogilvie said, "I'll think about it."

She gave him her cell number and showed him the door.

# FIVE

After he had been at the police station for a while, he realized he should have called first. A woman behind a glass wall asked him a lot of questions and told him to hold on for several minutes. It ended up being around a half-hour. He walked around a small waiting area with some dated magazines and overheard a family complaining about the whereabouts of their son who had been arrested. They were in the wrong place, but didn't know it.

Finally, the woman called him over and said, "Who are you again?"

"Daniel Bridger." It was the fourth time he had told her.

"Okay. Your brother was a homicide victim, right?"

"Yes."

"Someone is coming down for you."

A few minutes later he was greeted by a compact detective in plain clothes. He was well dressed for a city cop. Blue starched shirt and silk tie, navy blue slacks, high and tight Marine crewcut. A Beretta semi-automatic holstered at his waist.

"Mr. Bridger?"

"Yes."

"John Wilkening. I'm the detective assigned to this case." He gave Bridger a car salesman's handshake and direct eye contact, brief and firm.

Bridger followed him into a small elevator capable of holding about four people. As they went up the detective told Bridger he was sorry for his loss. Bridger nodded. The detective asked Bridger where he was from and Bridger told him Baltimore.

They sat at the detective's desk in an open area that was the homicide detectives' squad room. There were other detectives in plain clothes, a couple on the phone, a couple of others talking shop. It was a strange thing for Bridger, sitting in a police station, not being the subject of the investigation.

Detective Wilkening said, "Who notified you?"

"His girlfriend," Bridger said.

"No one from the department?"

"No," Bridger said. "So what happened?"

"Your brother was visiting one of his offenders at an apartment complex and he

45

was shot several times. We don't have any suspects yet, no persons of interest."

"It was in the parking lot of an apartment complex."

"Yes."

"Were there any video cameras around?"

"No."

"And no witnesses?"

"No, sir."

"Have your detectives questioned the residents of the complex, asked them what they saw or heard?"

"We had officers do a canvass, yes."

"Officers."

"Yes."

"But not detectives."

"It's the same thing on a canvass."

"How many officers?"

"I don't know at this time."

"Who was he visiting?"

"At the apartment complex?"

"Yes."

"Well, that's in the report. We got a statement from her."

"What's her name?"

The detective looked at Bridger uneasily. "Why do you want to know?"

"I'd like to talk to her."

The detective made a point of sighing, looking at his report and then looking at

Bridger. He said, "Mr. Bridger, what is it you do for a living?"

"I'm a mechanic. I own a repair shop in Baltimore. We do some restoration work too."

"I presume you have no experience in law enforcement."

"That's right."

"Why don't you leave it to us, then?" A patronizing tone, the cop in him coming out now.

Bridger said, "Okay. What do you guys *think* happened?"

"We think it was a robbery, plain and simple. Unfortunately, some of these apartment complexes are filled with gangsters. They saw a target and they killed him and took his money. It's not uncommon."

"Not uncommon to rob a cop?"

"You're presuming they knew he was a cop. He wasn't one, actually. He was a probation and parole officer. Which is not the same thing."

"I understand he was carrying a firearm."

"That's correct."

"And was he driving his personal vehicle?"

The detective looked down at his report, as if the answer would be on the page he was looking at. Making a show of it. Then he said, "I don't believe so. I believe it was

47

a state vehicle."

"So this robber, he was bold enough to rob an armed parole officer driving a state car."

"Well, some of these guys, they're so stoned or cranked out they don't think about things like that. Can you understand that?" A little hardness in his tone now.

"Sure," Bridger said. "But what I don't understand is why a crackhead would kill him and take his wallet and not take his gun."

The detective said nothing.

Bridger said, "Has that bothered you?"

The detective made a short, fake laugh. He said, "Mr. Bridger, I can understand your being upset. But I assure you we're doing all we can."

Bridger nodded and said, "What about the other offenders he was supervising? Have you checked into them?"

"We will, I assure you." The detective took a card from his desk and handed it to him. He stood up and said, "If you need anything, feel free to call me."

Bridger was being dismissed. He accepted it and stood up. The detective extended his hand again. Bridger shook it again and walked out.

# SIX

The attendant at the morgue asked him for his identification. She looked at the photo and looked back at him. She handed the driver's license back to him and directed him to sit on a bench in the lobby. He waited until another attendant wearing blue scrubs came and escorted him past the autopsy room to the storage area. Bridger could smell it, the damp, chemical odor of the dead. They got to the hall where there were a set of box-size steel drawers, reminiscent of old Dewey Decimal boxes at the library. The coroner's assistant told them they had finished the autopsy yesterday. He said the autopsy showed that the two bullets fired into the victim's face had killed him.

The coroner's assistant stopped at the second drawer and turned and said, "The body's already been identified. Are you sure you want to do this?"

"Yeah," Bridger said.

The coroner's assistant pulled the drawer open.

His brother's body was covered with a blue sheet up to the waist. The blue sheet was the same color as the coroner's assistant's scrubs. Seth's skin was gray, not ghoulish but not human either. His face was unrecognizable, punctured and destroyed by gunfire. *It's not him,* Bridger thought. It's a corpse, a cadaver. It was not his brother. It was no longer human because the soul had left. He looked down the length of the body and saw the feet sticking out of the sheet at the other end. There was a tag tied to the toe, the tag reading, *Bridger, Seth.*

Bridger closed his eyes, an involuntary reflex.

"Okay," he said.

The coroner slid the body back into its slot.

He checked into a hotel about a mile from Pike's Market. He had to park his car in a garage three blocks away. The hotel had been built in the twenties. It had two small elevators and a lobby that looked out onto an intersection. His room was small and modest. It was stuffy, so he opened a window to air out the room. He heard the sounds of traffic and light rain.

He took the yellow pages out of the desk drawer, looked up a number and dialed a number for a funeral home.

"Hello . . . Daniel Bridger. My brother's died . . . Seth Bridger . . . no, no other kin . . . His body is at the county morgue . . . I'd like him picked up tomorrow . . . I'll be paying for it. Yes, I have Visa . . . No, we won't need a wake . . . Yes . . . yes. Thank you."

The assistant at the funeral home asked him what he would like put on the tombstone.

Bridger thought of Seth's girlfriend. She would be able to answer that question better than he would.

Bridger said, "I don't know yet. I'll call you later with that information."

He hung up the phone and lay on the bed and looked up at the ceiling and thought back to the smell of the morgue. His little brother's body on a slab, the indignity of such a death. His brother had been a stranger to him. He had allowed it, and maybe Seth had allowed it too. Yet he looked at a corpse and saw his own blood, his brother, age thirty-two, murdered, his life stolen from him.

Bridger squeezed his eyes shut and covered them with his arm. He remained that way for a long time.

# SEVEN

The ADS (Assistant District Supervisor) of the county probation and parole office was a woman named Ann Tipken. She was heavy and irritable and she looked like she didn't want to spend too much time with him. Bridger said he just wanted to ask a few questions about his brother's work. ADS Tipken said they weren't in charge of the investigation.

Bridger asked, "Well, can I at least get his personal things out of his desk?"

The ADS sighed and told him to wait a minute. She walked to the receptionist's desk and dialed a number. She got someone on the line and Bridger heard her mutter, "Well, I don't know what to do with him. . . . No one told me anything. . . . Chris? . . . Well, all right."

She got off the receptionist's phone and said, "Come with me."

She pressed her identification card against

a red light that unlocked the door and pushed herself through it. Bridger followed her to an elevator as she turned to him and said, "I don't do stairs." In the elevator he was closer to her than he would have liked. They got off the elevator and walked to a room of gray desks and old carpet and non-uniformed civil servants. There were four of them sitting at their desks, a woman standing by another desk. The woman was around forty. She wore a blue jacket with the probation and parole logo on the breast, her sleeves rolled up to her elbows, a semi-automatic pistol at her waist. The woman was short and a little buxom. She didn't wear makeup and she had a strong-looking face with high cheekbones, suggesting a hint of Cherokee. Her hair was blonde and cut short. She extended her hand to Bridger.

"I'm Chris Rider. I worked with your brother."

Bridger shook her hand. "Dan," he said.

"Your brother was a good man."

"Thank you."

The ADS woman said, "You got it?"

Chris Rider gave the ADS a look. "Yeah, I got it."

The ADS walked off and Chris said, "Sorry."

"That's okay."

"Well, it's really not." She stared a couple of holes into the ADS's back and then brought them back to Bridger. She said, "I brought a box and started putting his things into it. But I thought maybe I'd leave that to you."

She gestured to the chair at the desk and Bridger sat in it. She said, "I guess I'm supposed to watch you, make sure you don't take any government property. You know, like paper clips or a stapler."

"It's okay," Bridger said. He started opening drawers.

Chris Rider said, "I'm glad you're here. I mean, I'm glad you're here rather than his girlfriend."

"Why is that?"

"I think this might be kind of tough on her. I know she was in love with him."

"Yeah?" Bridger said. "What did he think about her?"

He looked up at her after he said it. The woman was looking down at him, a curious, almost shocked expression.

Chris said, "You don't know?"

"No. I don't."

"He was nuts about her. He was going to marry her."

"Yeah, she told me that."

"Why didn't you believe her?"

"Who says I didn't?"

The probation and parole officer was looking at him now like she was unsure of him.

Bridger started to put photos in the box. He saw a calendar book and put that in the box too. He passed over a pair of nail clippers and a spare ink cartridge.

Chris said, "When was the last time you spoke to him?"

"To who?"

"Your brother."

A couple of parole officers drifted up to the desk. A black guy and a white guy. Chris Rider said, "This is Seth's brother. Is it Dan?"

"Yeah. Dan Bridger."

The white guy introduced himself as Tony Codespote. The black guy said he was Marlon Gage. Both of them extended their hands.

Marlon Gage said, "I'm really sorry, man. Your brother was a good officer."

"Thanks," Bridger said.

Gage said, "Anything you need, you let me know."

"I will, thanks."

The men drifted off, leaving Officer Rider alone with him.

She said, "I was asking you, when was the last time you talked with your brother?"

"I don't remember." He really didn't.

The woman stared at him again. She said, "You don't know, do you?"

"Know what?"

"Did Elaine tell you?"

"Tell me what?"

"She's two months pregnant."

Bridger stopped, looked up again.

Chris said, "Your brother was going to be a father. Didn't she tell you?"

"No. Is she still going to have it?"

The woman shook her head. She said, "God, no wonder he wrote you off. Are you about through?"

"Yeah, just about." Bridger smiled. "Seth wrote me off?"

"I don't want to discuss it. Seriously, are you about done?"

"Yeah." Bridger stood up, his hands on the box. He looked at the parole officer and said, "Can you take a break?"

"What for?"

"Because I'd like to talk to you. About him."

"I'm very busy."

"Please."

He gave her a look that demonstrated enough humanity. He didn't push it. He just put it out there.

"All right," she said. "Fifteen minutes."

In the parking lot, she told him she had to do some home visits but before that, they could stop for a drink at a bar and have a short discussion. Short, she stressed. She told him he could follow her in his car.

She got into a white Chevy Impala and he followed her in the Lincoln. When they got to the parking lot of a rundown-looking bar, she met him at the entrance. She said, "You can get coffee here, if you want. I just didn't want to go to a coffee shop. They're so . . . Seattle."

Bridger asked, "What do you mean?"

"I don't know. My dad used to work for Boeing. That was back when this was a blue-collar town. Now it's for the super rich."

"Why stay then?"

"It's my home. Where else would I go?"

He followed her into the dive bar that had little windows at the front that you couldn't see in or out of. The bar was smoky and Patsy Cline was on the jukebox. They took seats in a booth and she ordered a Diet Coke. Bridger was not surprised to see her light a cigarette. Bridger ordered a Coke. The cocktail waitress shook her head as she walked off.

Chris Rider said, "I have to go back on duty. What's your excuse?"

"I don't drink."

"Recovering alcoholic?"

"No. I just quit a long time ago. I don't have the stomach for it."

The woman shook her head. Either it surprised her or she didn't believe him.

Bridger said, "What I was talking about earlier, I wasn't saying that my brother's girlfriend should have an abortion. I was just asking."

"Why don't you ask her?"

"She didn't tell me about it."

"So you met her."

"Yes."

"What did you think of her?"

"She was okay."

"What do *you* think she should do?"

"I don't know. It's none of my business, I guess."

"None of your business. It's your brother's child."

Bridger shrugged.

"Jesus, you're a cold one. You're nothing like him."

"That's good to hear."

The woman said nothing.

"Look," Bridger said, "I'll help her out. I can. I have some money."

"What do you do?"

"I own a garage."

"And business is good?"

"Good enough. I'll help her."

The waitress returned with their sodas. The jukebox changed records. Jerry Jeff Walker singing now.

Chris Rider said, "Is that why you wanted to talk to me? To tell me you have money?"

Bridger said, "I met with the homicide detective investigating the murder. He wasn't very helpful."

"No?"

"He said he thinks Seth was killed by a mugger. But I'm not sure about that. You see, whoever killed him didn't take his gun."

"And that bothers you?"

"Yeah."

"You have any background in law enforcement?"

In different company, Bridger might have smiled or laughed. He didn't now. He said, "Not much."

"Yet you feel comfortable second-guessing a detective?"

"It just seems strange to me, that's all. What do you think?"

"Yeah, I guess it's a little strange. But most of these people are so high they don't know what they're doing. Criminals aren't rational people."

"So it's just random?"

"I don't know."

Bridger said, "Haven't you thought about it?"

"Of course. Look, the police are handling it. It's only been a couple of days. They'll find the killer."

"What about your office?"

"What about it? Are you saying we should do an investigation?"

"Why not?"

"We're not an investigating agency. This is a probation and parole office. Some people think we shouldn't even be allowed to carry firearms. You know anything about this kind of work?"

He had actually never been on probation. He had served all of his sentence way back when.

"No," he said.

"There's always a tension between people who see this as social work and people who see it as an extension of law enforcement. I'm not sure where I stand. On the law enforcement side, we've got our share of cowboys. Always looking for a reason to arrest the clients. Those are the guys that wanted to be cops but somehow weren't able to. I'm not one of them, if that's what you're thinking."

"I wasn't thinking that."

"Okay. Anyway, the problem is, the state doesn't really want us to arrest people on probation. They say they do, but they don't really want it. The prisons are too full. We can build more prisons, but that would mean raising taxes and who wants to pay higher taxes for that?"

"Where did Seth stand?"

"He was no cowboy. He saw it as social work and he was okay with that."

"But he carried a gun."

"Well, he had to. Some of these offenders can be rough. Particularly if they're cranked."

"He was in law school."

"Yeah, that's right. He would have finished in two years. That was his ticket out."

"What about you? You trying to get out?"

"If only." She paused, pulled on her cigarette. "Oh, it's not that bad. The benefits are good. In three years, I'll have my twenty in and I can draw a full pension. Civil service mentality. But that wasn't Seth. He was different."

"Do you think one of the people he was supervising may have killed him?"

Chris Rider sighed. "It's possible, I guess. But . . . I don't know. It's very, very rare that an offender kills his parole officer."

"They're not violent?"

"Some of them are plenty violent. But I've been here seventeen years and I've never heard of a parole officer being murdered by one of his clients."

"You call them clients."

"Offenders, clients. Depends on your point of view, I guess."

"Have the homicide detectives questioned you?"

"No."

"Have they asked for a list of Seth's clients?"

"Not to my knowledge." She looked at him warily. "Is that the real reason you asked me to talk to you? To get that list yourself?"

Bridger shrugged.

Chris Rider shook her head. "Forget it. I give you that, they'll fire me."

Bridger said, "Don't you want to know?"

"Who killed Seth? Of course I do."

Bridger regarded her. He said, "What was he to you?"

"He was a friend. That's all." She looked away and for a while didn't say anything. Then she shook her head. "Okay," she said, "I liked him. Maybe a little more than he liked me. I once asked him to have a couple of beers with me after work. He came with me, thinking it was just a friend thing, but after awhile he figured out that I was — that I liked him. But . . . I could tell he wasn't interested. Not in the way I was interested in him." She paused. "I guess I am a little older than him."

"Not so much."

"Thanks," she said, giving him a funny look. "I guess. But he was a gentleman about it. He was nice."

Bridger thought of the girl in the apartment with the red table and the large brown sweater hiding the beginnings of her child. He said, "He probably wasn't your type anyway."

"You didn't even know him," Chris said. "How would you know what his type was?"

"I guess I wouldn't."

"You don't know what my type is either."

Bridger said nothing. He liked her. He liked her look and her manner. He liked her figure and the way she held a cigarette and the way her gun rode on her hip and the way she spoke short to him. He wouldn't have turned her down and he suspected she probably knew that too.

"Look," she said, "I have to get back to work." She stood up.

Bridger said, "Can I call you?"

64

"What for?"

"I'm planning his funeral. I think he'd want you there."

Her face scrunched up and she almost broke. But then she stopped it and pushed it back and said, "Is there any other reason?"

"Maybe I'll want your help too."

"Yeah, that's what I thought."

She handed him her card and walked out.

# EIGHT

The windshield wipers were set on intermittent, pushing off the spitting rain. Clearing the windshield and resting then clearing again. The view of the gray and black street opening up to the two men inside the vehicle.

They were police officers, dressed in plain clothes. The vehicle was a black Dodge Charger with dark plexiglass covers on the headlights, giving the relatively new vehicle a retro look. In the driver's seat was a man named Charles Eatherly. He was in his early thirties, a tall black guy with about two hundred pounds on his frame. The man sitting next to him weighed about the same, though he was five years older. He was also black, but, unlike Eatherly, there was no blubber on him. He was well muscled and well defined. He looked like an athlete because he was one. He had once been one of the most promising wide receivers in high school football, his name and face in *Parade Magazine*. But when he graduated high school, none of the major college programs outside of the Pacific Northwest expressed much interest in him. The University of Washington passed and the Oregon Ducks didn't call him back after his tryout. He played for a small college in Spokane but hurt his knee his sophomore year. He didn't finish school there. Years later he got a degree from a state university in Seattle. His name was Dean Coates and he held the rank of sergeant with the Seattle PD.

Eatherly was a corporal. They were both operatives in the Special Investigative Unit (SIU), a tactical group formed two years earlier. Dean Coates was in charge of the unit.

There were three other officers in the unit — Patterson, Hammond, and Dupree. Most of them had had experience working as undercover narcotics agents.

Eatherly had the radio on a hip-hop channel. Coates told him to turn it down as he lifted his cell phone to his ear.

Coates now calling his wife.

"Hey," Coates said. "How you doing? . . . That's good . . . I won't be home for dinner tonight . . . I know, I know . . . put Greg on."

Greg, his thirteen-year-old son.

Coates with more of a smile in his voice now, saying, "Hey man. How was track practice? . . . Yeah?" Laughing at something his boy said. "Now I don't want to hear that . . . yeah . . . you be good to your sister or you'll be dealing with me, little man." His voice softening a little. "Okay. I'll see you soon. Put your mama back on."

Now back with the voice he used with his wife. He said he would call her later.

Coates clicked the cell phone off and reached forward to change the station on the radio. He made a sort of grunting sound of disapproval at the sound of hip-hop. He ignored Eatherly's protesting "hey" and pressed the memory switch to his favorite station. Classical music began pouring out of the speakers. A quick plinking of a piano.

"Now that's music," Coates said.

A moment passing, then Eatherly said, "You really like this?"

"Yeah," Coates said. "I played a little piano in high school. You didn't know that, did you?"

"No."

"You know what this is?" Coates asked. "It's Mozart. The *Turkish March*."

Coates pulled another cell phone out of his pocket. This one was yellow. His family

68

one was blue. It made it easier when you picked different colors.

He turned slightly in his seat so that Eatherly wouldn't hear the voice on the other end of the line.

Tulie said, "Hey."

"Hi," Coates said.

"What are you doing?"

"Working." Coates's tone was a little smoother now. It was the voice he used with girlfriends. The light and easy voice he used in the first few months as they were still getting to know each other and hadn't reached the point where the woman had got on his nerves . . . Coates sensing something bothering Tulie now, Coates being solicitous and thoughtful as he asked what was wrong.

Tulie said, "What's wrong is I'm working with assholes. I've got one old bitch here who's about eighty and she's threatening to go home unless we don't get her some relief. My manager is holding me responsible for last month's low sales figure, like the recession is my fault. Someone ordered one of these jewelry boxes and now that it's here she says it's not what she ordered."

Coates said, "Is it?" He didn't know what else to say.

"Fuck, yes." Frustrated now, close to tears. Coates wished he had called later.

He said, "Well . . . that's not right."

"No. You don't treat people that way."

Coates didn't know who she was talking about now. The manager or the customer? He said, "No, you don't. Hey, you want me to come down there and straighten them out?"

"Come down and shoot 'em."

Coates laughed. "Maybe I will."

"Okay. I gotta go. I'm out of here about eight, should be home about eight-thirty. You coming by?"

"You know it. You need anything?"

"A bottle of wine. Silver Oak. Can you remember that?"

It would probably be at least forty dollars. *Well,* Coates thought, *you asked.* He said, "I'll try."

"I'll see you tonight," Tulie said and hung up.

Tulie Yoon was tall for an Asian. She was long legged and full breasted and arguably a little thick in the hips. But Coates liked the package. He didn't like women who were too skinny. Looked too much like boys modeling designer jeans. He had met Tulie at a party hosted by some guy who used to do promotion work for the Sonics before they left for Oklahoma City and changed their names to something else. Tulie said

70

she was a dancer but she had to sell gifts and wares at a department store in Redmond. She said she spoke three languages and a little Italian because she had once spent a summer in Verona. She had been Coates's girlfriend for a few months. He liked the way she looked on his arm and he liked her body and her cruel smile and the way you never knew quite what she was going to say. He liked the way she could be coldblooded sometimes in the way she looked at things. She knew things about art and books that he didn't know and he liked that too. She had an eye for fashion, a good sense of what worked for her and on her. She liked to look good. And she had a preference for Italian things. She told him that she could have been a very successful clothes designer, but something seemed to get in the way. The Italian boots Coates had bought her cost about four hundred dollars and that was with her employee discount. The Gucci bag, that was another seven hundred. Six fifty for the three pairs of designer jeans. And there was that black wool weather coat from Norway or France with the zippers that went up the sides — two thousand with tax. She would never beg him for these gifts. She would never plead. She would just sort of point them out and say she really liked it and if that didn't get the point across, she might look him in the eye and say, "You think you can handle that?"

Eatherly knew not to ask him about his girlfriends.

Now they pulled up to a tall set of dank apartments. Off white with black iron balconies. They got out of the Charger and walked through the cracked glass doors of the lobby. The locks had been knocked off the lobby door long ago. Children ran around the area in the back where there was no playground. Coates and Eatherly took the elevator to one of the upper floors.

They got off the elevator and walked down a poorly lit corridor to an apartment near the end and knocked on the door. They heard no answer and Eatherly said, "Open up or I'll break this motherfucker *down.*"

A young black man with a do-rag opened the door.

"Hey, Dean," the young man said.

The young man, whose name was Lukas, held up a fist for Coates to knock down. Coates did it and walked in. Lukas did not extend his fist to Eatherly.

Another young black man sat in a black leather recliner watching television. The huge television was a nice new flat screen with high def. On the screen, Jim Brown was in Army fatigues lying on a military cot, Lee Marvin trying to talk him into dying for his country.

The young black man in the recliner was about twenty. He was compact of build, tight and fully muscled. He had been on his high school wrestling team and once came in second in a state championship. A distant memory for him now. His name was Billy Hicks, but most of his friends called him Hambone.

Coates stood in the room, forming a triangle of sorts with Hambone and the television. Coates looked from the television to Hambone and then back again. Eatherly stood a little bit behind Coates.

Hambone was making a point of ignoring Coates, keeping his eyes focused on the movie. Coates went along with him, playing it out.

Coates said, "Mister Jim Brown. The greatest football player ever lived."

Hambone nodded. Not making eye contact.

Coates said, "You know something? He was also one of the greatest lacrosse players ever to play the game. That's right. He's in the pro football hall of fame *and* the lacrosse hall of fame."

Hambone shrugged. Like, so fucking what?

And Coates had to admit that got to him a little bit. Boy not showing respect for Jim Brown.

Coates smiled, a cold smile. He said, "You seen Jeffrey?"

Hambone said, "What?"

"I said have you seen Jeffrey?"

Hambone said, "No I ain't seen no goddamn Jeffrey. What do I look like, a GPS? I tell you what, you see Jeffrey, send him to me. Nigger owes me two hundred dollars. And I need my money."

Hambone was smiling now. Dean glanced over at Lukas. Lukas looking very nervous, wanting it to be over, wishing Hambone would show some respect.

Coates asked, "When do you expect him back?"

"I told you, I don't know." Putting a little bone in his voice now.

Coates said, "Charles."

Charles Eatherly walked over and picked the television up. He pulled it away from the stand, jerking the electrical cord and cable out of the wall, carried it out to the balcony, Hambone saying, "Hey, hey!", as Eatherly dropped it off the balcony.

Eatherly remained at the balcony and

watched it as it went down to the ground and smashed into a million pieces.

Hambone was on his feet now, shocked that they had done it. Three thousand dollars' worth of television in little bits. He stared at Dean Coates, debating a rush.

Coates's handgun was at his side. Showing, but his hand wasn't on it. Coates eyes bored into Hambone's. Coates wanting him to try something.

Coates said, "Oh, I'm sorry. Were you watching that?"

Hambone said, "I told you, I don't know where he is."

Coates said, "He's behind."

"He's going to pay you. Why the fuck you got to bust my shit? That wasn't his."

"You living with the man. Maybe he's got a share in that television too."

"He doesn't."

"You're part of his crew," Coates said. "What have you got?"

"I don't have anything."

"Narcotics intel says you do. Between the two of you, you're clearing three thousand a week selling crack. And that's just on this corner."

"Shit."

"We got you on tape. I want fifteen hundred. Tomorrow."

"Man, we don't have it."

"You're lying to me. And if you're not, well you can get it by tomorrow."

Eatherly said, "Otherwise, I'll throw both your asses off a here."

Coates said, "Brother, let me remind you: I'm being reasonable. Fifteen hundred total. That's seven fifty from each of you. That's a small price to pay to stay in business. Wouldn't you say?"

Hambone looked at the two cops and then looked at himself through their eyes. A punk they could kill or put in jail. Sergeant Coates wanting an answer to his question now.

Hambone said, "Yeah." His tone subdued.

"That's what I thought."

The police officers started to leave, Eatherly stopping in front of Hambone to put his hand to Hambone's face, a violating touch. "Tomorrow, little man," Eatherly said.

Coates said, "You boys take care, now."

Outside, there were a handful of people gathered around the broken pieces of the television. The cops walked by, not acknowledging it.

In the car, Coates gave a little lecture to Charles about calling Hambone "little man." Coates said it was okay to break the man's television, the bitch had it coming for giving them attitude, but calling the man little was a diss. Charles said how was one okay and not the other? Coates said there was a line. The line was sometimes hard to define, but you had to try to see it.

Coates said, "See, you call the man little, you insult him. The other thing, you're just making a point. He knows the difference."

Eatherly said, "I don't understand that."

Coates said, "What I'm saying is, you don't want to put the man in a position where he feels he has to do something to get his respect back. Then he might come at you and I'll have to shoot him or you'll have to break something of his. Then we don't get our money."

Eatherly made a gesture. "It's a point."

One of Coates's cell phones rang. He answered it.

It was Gage, saying he needed to talk to him as soon as possible.

Coates said, "You see that place? Ten years ago it didn't even have a sign. Well, not like the big sign they got there now. It was just a little theater. I had to work vice for a couple of weeks. Go in there, wait for the homos to pull it out and show it to me. Most of them old white men who were married. They'd say things like, 'What do you think of that? Do you like that?' One of them called it his willie. He was an Englishman or something. I arrested him for solicitation and he kept saying, 'Terribly sorry. Terribly, terribly sorry.' Almost felt sorry for the man."

Marlon Gage said, "Was that after you worked narcotics?"

"No. Before. Like I said, it was just for a few weeks. You'd sit in the theater or sometimes you'd sit in the stall in the bathroom, wait for a guy to slide his foot over. Give you a signal."

"That's gross," Gage said.

They were parked in Gage's car across the street from the porn theater. The rain was on full now, coming down in sheets. It made Coates feel better. It was hard to see in the rain.

Coates said, "So the man has a brother."

"Yeah," Gage said. "Daniel Bridger. From the East Coast. I ran an NCIS on him. Dean, he's got a record."

"Big time?"

"Not on paper. Did a few years in the Indiana state pen for breaking and entering. But . . . I don't know."

"What don't you know?"

"I saw him. He makes me nervous. He doesn't seem like a small-timer to me.

Something about the way he moves."

"Isn't that a song?"

"Pardon?"

"Never mind. He makes you nervous, I believe you."

"I'm not saying I'm scared of the man. I didn't *say* that. What I'm saying is the man's got a look of determination."

"You like to operate by feel, don't you?"

"Sort of. It wouldn't bother me to say I get feelings about things. Like, when you go into an offender's house, sometimes you know the guy's got a gun. Or he's up to something. I trust my inner voice. And right now, it's not very happy."

"I hear you. I suppose it's fair to say you'll be glad to see the back of this man?"

"That would be fair to say, yes."

"When is he leaving?"

"Chris says he's hanging around to plan a funeral. Apparently, this brother was the only family he had."

"What did she say the man does?"

"She says he's a mechanic. An auto mechanic."

Coates said, "Would you feel better if I did some checking on him? See if there's more to him than this B&E conviction?"

"It might cheer me up."

"All right," Coates said. "How's the family?"

"Good. My little girl's birthday is coming up. Sixteen years old and she wants a car. A new one."

"They grow up fast," Coates said. "I'll be in touch."

# NINE

The uniformed officer brought out a box and set it on the counter. He pulled items out of the box and began checking them against a list that he had printed out from a computer. They were Seth's things: his clothes, his keys, and his gun. The gun was a little black .38 Smith and Wesson snub-nose airweight. It was loaded.

The uniformed officer asked Bridger to sign the log. He did not hand Bridger a receipt. Bridger carried the box out to his rental car. The morning skies had started out clear, but by nine gray skies had moved in and brought the rain with them. In the car Bridger took the gun out of the box and put it in his coat pocket. He reached into his other coat pocket for the piece of paper where he had written down the girl's cell number. He got out of the car and walked to a pay phone.

■ ■ ■ ■

He saw Elaine Ogilvie get out of a used Isuzu Trooper. He watched her through the glass of the coffee bar as she walked toward him. She was wearing jeans, a T-shirt, and a raincoat. Looking better now than she did before. She didn't look pregnant, but it was hard to tell. She didn't carry an umbrella and didn't seem to care that her hair got wet.

She waved at him through the window, then came in and sat down across from him.

"Hello," Bridger said. "Thanks for coming."

"I didn't go to Spokane," she said. "We have final exams soon. I need to stay here and prepare for them."

"Okay."

"Not that I feel I should have to explain it to you."

"Sure. Can I buy you something?"

She seemed to relax a little, taking the strap of her bag off her shoulder. "Okay," she said. Bridger signaled the waitress. Elaine Ogilvie ordered a café au lait.

The waitress left and Bridger said, "I called a funeral home and made arrangements for a funeral. I don't want to schedule it without talking to you first."

"So I can come?"

"I wanted to check with you."

"Before you told me I should go stay with my parents. Now you're telling me to stay for his funeral."

"I haven't told you what to do. I just wanted to . . ."

"Keep me in the loop?" She smiled grimly. "Thanks."

Bridger didn't say anything.

The girl's expression softened. "Seriously," she said. "Thanks."

Bridger said, "They asked me what to put on the tombstone. I thought I should talk to you about it first."

The girl stared at him for a while. Then she said, "Oh. Well, I don't know."

"Give it some thought. And let me know what you want to do. I mean, I think you should . . ."

"I know what you mean. Thank you."

The waitress brought the café au lait, steaming out of a big yellow cup. Bridger noticed there was no cute swirl on the top of it.

Bridger placed the set of keys on the table. He said, "These are his. I guess there are the keys to your apartment."

Elaine looked at them. "They are," she said.

"And there are a set of car keys too. Are they to your SUV?"

"No. He had his own car."

"Was it paid off?"

The girl smiled. "I would hope so. It's an old car."

"What kind?"

"A Chrysler. Older than me."

"He liked old cars?"

"Yeah."

"Where is it now?"

"In the garage behind our apartment. You want it?"

"No. It belongs to you."

"Well I wouldn't know what to do with it."

"Sell it."

"I don't think it's worth anything."

"Maybe I'll buy it from you."

"If you want," she said.

Bridger said, "I met with the detective investigating the case. Do you mind if I talk to you about it?"

"No."

"He said more or less what you said. That they suspect it was a young gang member robbing him for his money."

"What did you think?"

"Of the detective?"

"Yes."

"I wasn't very impressed with him."

"You know much about police officers?"

"I know a few things. His name is Wilkening. Is he the one who talked to you?"

"Yes."

"Did he ask you any questions?"

"Not very many. He seemed to be interested in just telling me things."

Bridger said, "That was my impression too. He seemed like the sort of cop who should be working in administration. Like a deputy chief. What I'm saying is, he didn't seem to be too street smart."

Bridger paused, looking at the young woman his brother loved. He waited for her to say something clever, like, *And you are?*

But she didn't. She said, "I get the feeling you don't think much of police officers."

"I've got nothing against them, one way or the other. I respect any man who's good at his work."

"And you don't think this one is good at his work?"

"I don't. I hope I'm wrong, though. I asked him what he thought about Seth not having his gun stolen. He didn't seem bothered by it."

"Why not?"

"He said the — the person who did it probably was stoned."

"Doesn't that make sense to you?"

"Maybe. But maybe it was something planned. Maybe by one of the people he was supervising. What I'd like to do is stay here for a few days and look into it. I wanted to see if that would be okay with you."

The girl looked at him for a moment, surprised to see that he meant it. She said, "Are you asking me?"

"Yeah."

The girl looked at him steadily and Bridger began to see what his brother had seen in her. A young woman in her early twenties, but not a girl. No silliness or immaturity to her.

Elaine said, "Yes, I'm okay with that."

"I'd like to come to his — to your apartment and look through his things."

"What for?"

"To see if he kept any notes about his work."

"Okay," Elaine said. "Let me get a to-go cup."

At the apartment, she showed him to the bedroom they did not use for sleeping. In the room was a futon in couch mode and a small computer workstation. Bridger gestured to the computer and said, "Is this yours or his?"

"It's ours. We both use it."

"Did he have another computer? A laptop?"

"He did, actually."

"Where is it?"

She went to the dining room, where it was sitting on the dining room table. She said, "It's in here."

He followed her voice. She was sitting at the table starting up the laptop. She got it going and stood up and offered him the chair. Bridger took it and she asked him if he wanted some coffee. He told her in a nice way he'd had enough coffee but wouldn't mind a glass of water. She went to the kitchen and brought back a bottle of the stuff.

Elaine remained standing behind him. A couple of minutes and she heard him say, "Okay."

Elaine said, "You found something?"

"Yeah. He kept a list of the offenders here. . . . It seems just like basic information. . . . Did he carry a notebook?"

"You mean, like a little one?"

"Yeah. The sort cops put in their pockets."

"He did."

Bridger turned and looked at her. He said,

"It wasn't in the box they gave me."

"The box — you mean the box with his possessions?"

"Yeah. The things he had on his person when it happened. It's not in the box. Have you seen it around here?"

"No."

Bridger turned back to the screen. He said, "Do you have a printer?"

"Yeah. In the study room. Do you want me to print that list out?"

"Yeah."

"Here. Let me send the document to my e-mail. Then I can print it out without having to hook up his computer."

"Okay. Do you mind if I look at the car?"

"You can take the car, I told you."

"Where is it?"

"In the garage out back. The door doesn't lock."

Bridger walked through the kitchen and down the back stairs. Into a small yard with a thin sidewalk leading to the gate. The yard next door had a clothesline and a little beagle that started barking at him.

Bridger opened the garage door and saw the back of a 1971 Chrysler 300. It had been a while since he had seen one of these. It was dark green with a white vinyl top. It had a couple of rust spots near the bottom and a little circle of rust around the key hole in the trunk. A big car with sofa-size seats in the front and back. Concealed headlights and a chrome lined grill. The car your grandma might have driven if her husband was middle management at a machine shop.

Bridger inspected it further. He opened the hood and looked at the 383 four-barrel big block motor. He got in and started it up.

It ran steady and the interior was in good shape. Seth must have bought it off an old lady who couldn't drive it anymore or from an estate. It must have been well kept and garaged because a car this age would have much more rust otherwise. It was a find. If they had known each other, Seth could have called him after he bought it and let him know what he had found. Told him he picked up an old four door Chrysler and he'd only paid about two grand for it. Something they could talk about at least for a while.

Bridger shut the car off and went back inside.

Upstairs, Elaine handed him the list of Seth's offenders.

Bridger folded it and put it into his pocket. He said, "I'm going to drop the rental off and take a cab back here and pick up the Chrysler. Is that all right with you?"

"You're not going to steal it, are you?"

Bridger looked at her for a moment.

"It was a joke," she said. "Sorry."

"No, that's all right. It was funny. I'd just like to drive it. I like older cars too. I just want to borrow it for a while."

She nodded at him in a way that almost reached him. He thought then about her baby and almost said something to her about it but then he decided not to.

She looked at him then, still unsure of what he was about, and she said, "Let me know what you find out."

"I will," Bridger said and left.

# TEN

Coates said he'd take one more question. A black girl on the fourth or fifth row asked if relations between the police department and "the community" had improved since he had become a policeman. The girl didn't say "black community" but Coates knew it was what she meant. He paused, timing it, and said, "Well, I tell you, I wouldn't want to be a part of a police department that didn't want to improve its community. That's the purpose behind my Neighborhood Community Outreach program." He looked at the young black girl and said, "I hear where you're coming from. I know. Thirty, forty years ago, police officers had some attitudes that were not, let's say, *beneficial* to the community. But things have changed. Crime hurts our community the most. The poorest people are the ones suffering the most. Police departments across the nation are becoming more progressive, and I'm happy to be part of that."

He left it at that. The assistant principal approached the podium and asked the students to thank Sergeant Coates. He got a nice round of applause. He smiled and waved as he walked off the auditorium stage.

The assistant principal was a Hispanic lady who gave him a nice smile and touched him on the arm as he left. Coates smiled back at her, thinking, yeah, maybe if she dropped about twenty pounds.

Coates liked speaking at high schools. Telling students his personal story: growing up on "the streets," his football career, how he learned to adapt, etc. He was aware of his good looks, his natural charisma, his ease with public speaking. He was also aware, to a degree, of his weaknesses. He could be a football coach at one of these high schools and be looked up to by the students and the athletes. But some of these girls wanted to grow up fast and when they'd come on to him, he'd find it very hard to resist. Too much temptation at a place like this.

He hung around backstage for a while as the assistant principal told him how much it meant to the kids to have such a good role model come and speak to them. How grateful they were to have him come here on his own time and how grateful *she* was too, adding "and I *mean* that," Coates smiling back at her, being gracious while thinking to himself, *Lady, it ain't gonna happen.*

In the parking lot he made a call. The man on the other end said he had some things to tell him and asked him if they could meet now. Coates said they could.

Alex had the throttles on full, pushing the boat through the waters of Lake Washington. The rain had dissipated, but the sky was still overcast and gray. Coates watched Alex Dupree at the helm. It was Alex's day off. Alex liked to be on his boat when he wasn't working. Alex wore an expensive navy blue anorak and jeans, boat shoes, and no socks. He dressed white on his days off and he didn't care who knew it. He kept the throttle maxed as he turned the wheel to the left, hurtling the boat around a turn, the boat sliding a little across the water. In heaven, he was, on his boat that Coates had helped him buy.

Alex slowed the boat and then cut the engine. They floated for a minute and Alex got a couple of cans of beer out of a cooler. He tossed one to Coates.

"Beautiful day," Alex said. "We could go up to Sheridan Beach, maybe see some girls."

"Probably start raining by the time we get there," Coates said. "What did you find out?"

Alex said, "You remember Lewis?"

"Pond?"

"No, not Pond, goddammit. Smith. Lewis Smith."

"Yeah. He got on the FBI."

"Right. When he finished at Quantico, they wouldn't let him work Seattle 'cause he grew up here. See, they don't like you working in the neighborhood you grew up in."

"I'm aware of that."

"Okay. Well, they sent him to Omaha. And he did not like that at all."

"Get to the point," Coates said.

"I'm getting there. So he put in about two years there and put in for a transfer to Chicago. Got that. And now he's much happier."

Coates looked at Alex for a while, wondered how many beers he'd had.

"Alex . . ."

"So," Alex said, "he works with a guy now who used to be in the Philadelphia field office. And he knew something about this man."

"Bridger?"

"Yeah. A couple of years ago, there was

94

some shit going on in Philadelphia. This Bridger was suspected of killing this judge. A home invasion. Apparently, this Bridger is a thief. And not just some smash-and-grab crank head motherfucker. Strictly high-end shit. Plans his work, works his plan."

"Go on."

"They believed he had broke into this judge's home and killed him and his wife. No, wait, it wasn't the wife. It was the judge's mistress. Both of them shot and killed. Turns out, though, this judge was dirty. Taking money from the Mob."

"Mob . . . ? Italians?"

"Yeah."

"Why didn't they arrest him?"

Alex shrugged. "Couldn't make the case. They later pinned it on this other dude, this mafia guy. But, get this, the mafia guy that set it up, he was killed too."

"By who?"

"Well, the official story is, he was killed by the Tessa family out of New York. But some cops think this Bridger did it, set it up in such a way that it looked like the mob did it. They *suspect* that but they couldn't prove it. What they *know* is, he killed three people working for this mafia guy."

"Why didn't they charge him for that?"

"Self-defense. The only witness left alive

was a woman who said he acted in his defense and hers."

Coates looked out north to Mount Rainier, the peak shrouded in mist. Coates said, "Three guys."

"Yeah," Alex said. "Just like that. Dean?"

"Yeah."

"What do you think?"

"Well," Coates said, "I don't know. Does it make you nervous?"

"Normally, I'd say no. But we got this deal coming up and it seems like we shouldn't have anything else to worry about. Know what I'm saying?"

"Yeah," Coates said, "we could take care of him, definitely. But that's gonna look suspicious, both of them dying in the same week. Say the man is a hard motherfucker. That doesn't mean he *knows* anything. You see?"

"Yeah, I see."

"I'll tell you what," Coates said. "You let me worry about Mr. Bridger."

# ELEVEN

A skinny guy said something ugly to a fat girl and then another skinny guy stood up and started toward him, both of them pulling off their shirts. Cuss words bleeped out as the audience cheered at the prospect of some violence. In the corner of the television set was the *Jerry Springer* logo.

Detective John Wilkening came into the police officers' break room where Bridger was watching television. Two more people were in there waiting to talk to detectives.

Wilkening said, "What are you doing in here?"

Bridger said, "They told me this was the waiting area."

"No, I mean, what are you doing back here?"

"I wanted to talk to you."

"I told you if I knew anything, I would call you. Didn't I tell you that?"

Detective Wilkening seemed a little hot

under the collar. Standing there in his pressed blue shirt and blue silk tie with an American flag lapel pin. Bridger looked back at him and wondered if he had been on patrol any more than two years.

Bridger said, "I found something out that I thought might help you."

"You're going to help me," Wilkening said, being sarcastic now.

Bridger said nothing.

Wilkening said, "Come back here. I want to talk to you."

Bridger followed him down a series of hallways. Then they were in a small room with no windows and a long table. An interrogation room. This was something familiar.

The detective gestured for Bridger to sit down, but did not order him to do it. Bridger and the detective took opposite seats at the table.

Wilkening said, "You haven't been honest with me, Mr. Bridger."

Bridger said, "What about?"

"About yourself. You have a criminal record."

"Yeah. Did I tell you I didn't?"

"I asked what you did. You said you were a mechanic."

"Right."

The detective waited for him to say something else. He didn't. The detective put on one of those cop disappointed schoolteacher looks and said, "If I'm going to help you, you need to tell me those things."

"What things?"

"What things. Things like your prior conviction for breaking and entering."

"That was over fifteen years ago. What does it have to do with this?"

"How about you tell me?"

Bridger believed the detective thought he was being pretty clever. *How about you tell me?* Sitting there in his crisp clothes, playing the part of the detective rather than doing any actual work. There were smart cops out there. Couldn't they have assigned one to this homicide?

"Mr. Wilkening, do you have some reason to suspect me for my brother's murder?"

"Now hold on there. If we're going to be getting into that, I have to read you your *Miranda* rights."

"I'll waive them, if you think it's necessary. So. Do you?"

"Do I . . . ?"

"Do you have any reason to suspect me in the murder of my own brother?"

"I didn't say that."

"I can give you my airline ticket. It'll tell you when I got to Seattle."

"That won't be necessary. Okay? There's no reason to go into that."

"Good," Bridger said. "Listen, I picked up Seth's possessions from the evidence room. They said they didn't need them anymore."

"Did you sign for them? You know you're supposed to sign for them."

Bridger stared at the detective for a moment. "Yes," he said. "I signed for them. He had a little notebook he carried with him for work. Notes he took during his home visits with the offenders. Maybe notes he took before and after the visits."

"Yeah. So what?"

"That notebook is missing."

"I see. Maybe he left it at home."

"His girlfriend has checked their apartment. She hasn't seen it."

"Maybe it's at his workplace."

"Maybe."

"Have you checked there?"

"No." Bridger decided to hesitate before speaking again. Then he said, "I thought maybe you might want to do that."

"You think it's significant that his notebook is missing. I mean, *might* be missing."

"Yeah. I thought it might mean something."

The detective smiled at him. Maybe trying to express sympathy for the dumb ex-con, maybe expressing contempt. Bridger didn't like it for any reason.

The detective said, "I'll look into it. Okay?" Like, will that make you happy?

Bridger made a gesture, saying that would be okay with him.

"But," Detective Wilkening said, "I'm going to have to warn you that this department doesn't solve every homicide. Some years, our rate is only around sixty percent. That means, forty percent of the homicides go unsolved."

Bridger said, "What about when the victims are law enforcement? I thought that might rate a higher priority than your average homicide."

"Your brother was not a cop. He was a parole officer. And that's not the same thing."

When he was a young man, Bridger had something of a temper. He had learned to control it over the years. Had learned to stay cool and in control, for self-control and discipline were the tools of his profession. But right now he wanted to reach across the table and grab John Wilkening's tie and drag him across the table and slap the living dogshit out of him. It might be worth a few months in county jail just to do it.

But that would shut the investigation down.

In a quieter voice, Bridger said, "I'm beginning to see that. Detective, let me speak clearly. I could give a flying fuck what you think about me. I did my time and I don't have to answer to people like you for it. But do not make the mistake of confusing my brother with me. He was clean. He deserves to have his killer caught and arrested. You put this on the back burner and I'll make you regret it."

"Are you threatening me?"

"I'm threatening to make a complaint about you. If we're being taped, the record will demonstrate that."

"You're welcome to try. I'm not afraid of you. Now get out."

# TWELVE

He parked the Chrysler between a ragged-out Monte Carlo and an old four-door Chevy. He locked the car and walked up the flight of stairs. On the second landing a couple of black kids stopped talking when he walked by and gave him hard looks. Bridger ignored them and kept going. He knocked on the apartment door several times but no one answered. He stood and listened for the sound of a television set or people talking but he didn't hear anything. He walked back down the stairs.

He started to the car, got halfway there, but turned around and walked around the apartment complex. It had stopped raining. There were a couple of other kids on the balconies, some of them looking down at him, others ignoring him. A voice called something out to him and he ignored that too.

He saw a collection of people near an old

swing set, a little boy sliding down the slide, spreading his legs at the bottom so his feet wouldn't land in the puddle left by the rain. Two black women sat on a bench nearby. One of the women in her twenties, the other in her forties. Bridger walked up to them, nodding his head at them in a nonthreatening way when they saw and acknowledged him.

Bridger looked at the younger one. "Are you Natoya Carter?"

The older woman said, "What do you want?"

Bridger said, "Are you?"

"It's all right, mama," Natoya said. "Are you the law?"

"No. My name is Bridger."

The young woman looked at him for a moment. She said, "You kin to Seth?"

"Yeah. His brother."

"Oh. I'm sorry."

The older woman said, "What do you *want?*"

"I won't take long," Bridger said. "My brother was killed in this parking lot after he left your apartment. Did you see anything?"

"No. I already told the police I didn't. I'm sorry it happened."

"Did a Detective Wilkening talk to you

about it?"

"Who?"

"Detective Wilkening. A white man, about so high. Balding, kind of uptight."

"Would he a been in uniform?"

"No."

"Then I don't think so. An officer in a uniform talked to me, wrote things down. Then another man, I think he was a sergeant? He talked to me too."

"Anyone else?"

"No."

"What do you think happened?"

"Sir, I don't know."

Natoya's mother got off the bench and walked over to her grandson. She took him by the hand and led him away.

Bridger said, "Is that what you told the police?"

"Yeah."

"Say it was someone in this apartment complex, say a gang member. Say you did see it happen. Would you tell the police?"

"I know what you're saying. But I didn't see nothing. Really."

"If you did and you reported it, they'd come after you, wouldn't they? And you still have to live here. You and your son."

"Yeah. But that don't mean I saw anything."

He heard the older woman behind him, her voice almost a shout. "Man, what do you want? She said she didn't see nothing, she didn't see nothing. She's telling you the truth, but you don't want to hear it."

Bridger looked over his shoulder. Grandma looking back at him, holding the little boy's hand.

The woman saying now, "If it was someone here, don't you think she'd know it by now? Everybody would know."

"If you knew, would you tell me?"

"Hell, no. You lost a brother and I'm sorry. But it doesn't have anything to do with her. Or us."

"How do you know? How are you so sure it wasn't someone in this complex?"

The grandmother said, "Because if it had been, she'd a been *warned*. She'd a been told not to say nothing. And that hasn't happened. Now leave us alone."

When Bridger got to the Chrysler, he saw a black man sitting on the hood. A couple more guys standing nearby. They were all young and hard looking, two of them displaying their gang colors. The third one wore a blue hoodie up over his head, sunglasses. His hands were in his pockets.

Bridger decided he would be the one to watch.

Bridger stopped a few feet in front of them, his legs set apart. A small thing, but letting them know he wasn't frightened.

"Something I can do for you?" Bridger said.

The man on the hood of the car said, "Looks like you made a mistake."

"Coming here?" Bridger said. He took a long, appraising look at all three of them, letting them know he wasn't that impressed. "No, I don't think so."

The guy on the car said, "Man talk like that, he's either very brave or very stupid."

"Yeah," Bridger said. "Or he's armed."

The man's eyes flashed down to Bridger's waist. It was covered by a rain coat. Maybe there was a gun stuck in the waistband of the pants or in the coat pocket, maybe not.

The man on the car said, "Shit. You ain't got nothing."

Bridger laughed and said, "You want to find out?" He nodded to the hooded man and said, "It'll be him first. Then him. Then you."

The man on the car was quiet for a while. Smiling back at the white man who was smiling at him. He said, "What do you want?"

"My brother was killed here. He was a parole officer."

"Lot of probation and parole officers come here. Lot of men here on probation."

"His name was Bridger."

"Don't know him."

"He know you?"

"He'd have no reason to."

"You know who killed him?"

"No."

"Then I guess we got nothing to talk about," Bridger said.

Another pause as the man on the car thought things over. Moments passed by and he gave a head signal to the guy in the hooded sweatshirt. He got off the car and walked away, the other two following him.

Bridger got into the Chrysler and started it. He pulled out of the parking lot and drove down the street. At the second stop sign he came to, he opened the glove compartment and took the revolver out and put it in the pocket of his raincoat.

He pulled the Chrysler into a 7-11. He bought a newspaper and a small soda. He put a lid on the soda and a straw through the lid. He walked out to the pay phone in the parking lot and made a call.

"Yeah."

"Walter?"

"Yeah. Dan? What's up?"

"I'm in Seattle."

"What are you doing out there? Never mind. Don't tell me."

Bridger said, "I need to buy a gun. Can you recommend someone out here?"

"Seattle, Washington . . . well . . . no, not really. I know someone in Tacoma."

"Is he straight? I don't want to deal with any mental cases."

"Yeah, he's straight. Let me contact him and get back with you. You got a number?"

Bridger gave him the number at the pay phone.

Walter said, "I'll try to be quick."

"I appreciate that," Bridger said and hung up.

He walked back to the Chrysler and got in and read the newspaper. Twenty minutes went by. Cars pulled in and out of the lot. Another eight minutes ticked by and by then Bridger was reading through the classified ads. If Walter's contact didn't work out, he would look for an estate sale and maybe see if he could find something to look into, though he would try to avoid getting a gun that way. He could go back to the gangsters at the apartment complex and see what sort of guns they might have to offer. But he didn't like doing business with gangsters, particularly when they were young and angry and were more interested in proving themselves than making a deal. If he had actually had the .38 on him back there and they had called his bluff, it would have been dicey. Five shots in the gun and he would have had to have been lucky to put down all three before they got a bullet in him. And even if he had pulled it off, the gun could be traced back to him. It was Seth's gun and the police department had given it to him.

The phone rang and Bridger got out of the car and walked over and answered it.

"Yeah."

"Dan?"

"Yeah, Walter."

"The guy's name is Farrell Hatch. He's a good guy. He's in a town between Tacoma and Olympia. A town called Busby. Four twelve Winthrop Drive. Shouldn't be hard to find once you're in the town. He's expecting you. It should take you about an hour and a half to get there."

"You didn't tell him my name, did you?"

"Dan." Walter sounded insulted.

"Sorry," Bridger said and hung up.

The address was on the corner of a town

110

strip. A rustic area with wood fronts and porches and slanted parking on the street. Bridger parked the Chrysler next to an old Chevy Apache pickup. Got out and looked at a diner that was called the Mossy Rock Café. Bridger thought that Walter may have made a mistake, but Walter didn't make mistakes. There was a screen door at the front, the second door open. Bridger walked in.

There were tables with red and white plastic covers and stools alongside a counter, not a bar. A couple of vintage Coca-Cola signs and a Marlon Brando photo that Bridger figured was from *The Wild One,* but they didn't go overboard with it. A young lady of about twenty-five was behind the counter. She called Bridger sir and asked him if he'd like to see a menu. She said he could sit at the counter or at a table, whatever he liked. Bridger sat at the counter and ordered a cup of coffee.

She brought him a white cup and saucer and poured the coffee for him. Bridger asked if Mr. Hatch was in. The girl nodded while she continued pouring the coffee for him. She looked at him, briefly, and went to the back of the store.

A man in his late fifties came back to the counter. He was tall and thin and he had gray hair in a ponytail and he looked like he had never sat behind a desk in his life. He stood behind the counter and looked Bridger in the eye.

Farrell Hatch said, "How you doing?"

"Good."

"Like an early dinner or maybe a piece of pie?"

"I like pie," Bridger said. "Apple or cherry, but not pumpkin or other kinds that don't have real fruit. I'm a friend of Walter's."

"I figured you might be. You can bring the coffee with you, if you like. Candy?"

The young woman whose name was Candy said, "Yeah?"

"Can you cut this gentleman a piece of cherry pie and make it to go?"

"Does he want ice cream with it?"

The gun dealer turned to Bridger. Bridger shook his head.

"Just straight, darling," Hatch said. "We'll be back soon."

Bridger followed the man to the back of the store and out the rear door. Bridger said, "Your daughter?"

"My wife," Hatch said. "Like the poet said, we 'gather the rose of love' while there's still time. Or words to that effect. You know poetry?"

"Not really."

"Too bad. Women love it."

They walked through the back lot to a steel workshop and garage. Farrell Hatch punched in a code that unlocked the automatic garage door. Inside the garage was an early model two-door Volvo with a rally light on the top. It was in the process of being restored. The other side of the garage was taken up with workbenches and projects.

Farrell Hatch said, "Was it handguns or a rifle you wanted? If it's machine guns, you're going to have to go elsewhere."

Bridger liked that. He said, "I was interested in a handgun. A 1911 .45, if you have it."

Hatch said, "I've got a Colt Army issue. Beautiful piece but it weighs a lot and won't fit well in your coat pocket. I've got a baby Glock that's had 2500 rounds through it and never jammed once." Hatch pulled a cloth out and laid it on the workbench. The cloth was smooth and clean. He took out the baby Glock and set it on top of the cloth.

Hatch said, "Here's another one. A Glock Model 27, forty caliber. A lot of cops use that. And here's what I like." He set another gun on the cloth. "Springfield Armory Compact 1911A1. Black matte alloy frame, wood grips. Use a Wilson Combat 7 round magazine and you're good to go."

"You got an extra magazine?"

"Yeah." Hatch put another one on the table. He said, "At fifteen yards you can keep all your shots in a two-inch grouping and that's shooting fast and loose. It'll shoot better than you will."

"You got rounds?"

"Two boxes. That should be enough."

"Yeah. I'd like a small revolver too. A .357 Smith and Wesson, if you have one."

"Two-inch or four-inch?"

"Two."

"Ohhhkay." Hatch placed a .357 revolver on the table. Then he placed two boxes of rounds on the table next to it.

Bridger checked out both guns. They were clean and well taken care of. He checked their weight and balance. He said, "I'll take them both. And the rounds. What do I owe you?"

Farrell Hatch said, "Understand it's not just the guns you're buying, it's my time and my assurance that they're not going to get you in trouble."

"I got your name." It meant that Bridger had been assured Hatch had a reputation for not selling hot guns that had already been used to kill someone. That Hatch was a professional.

"Good," Hatch said. "It's going to be nine

hundred for the .45. Seven hundred for the revolver. Another hundred for the ammunition."

Bridger nodded and counted out seventeen hundred dollars in fifties.

Hatch picked up the money. Hatch placed the guns in separate boxes and put them with the shells in a cardboard box. He handed the box to Bridger.

Hatch said, "Thank you, sir. Your coffee and pie? Comped."

"I'm obliged," Bridger said.

Bridger put the guns in the trunk of the Chrysler and left.

# THIRTEEN

He heard a tap on the window and he looked over to see who it was.

He rolled down the window.

Chris Rider said, "You stalking me?"

He had parked in the lot of her office and sat and waited for her. Sometime, he had fallen asleep.

Bridger said, "I thought you might be getting off work now."

She said, "I recognized his car. What are you doing with it?"

"It's a good car."

"It gets about twelve miles to the gallon. Maybe fifteen on the highway."

"He tell you that?"

"Yeah."

Bridger said, "You buy a new energy-efficient car, it'll cost you about thirty thousand. A car like this isn't gonna use thirty thousand dollars' worth of gas if you keep it fifteen years."

The parole officer's voice was dry. "Is that right?"

"And that doesn't count the energy used to make a new hybrid."

"Think these things out, do you?"

"I guess I've had time."

"The people of Seattle aren't going to see things your way, environmentally speaking. They'd like to see these things taken off the road. Have you got something to tell me?"

"I was hoping we could talk."

"I can't be seen riding in this car with you. You being an ex-convict and all."

"Right. Can we meet somewhere? I'll even buy you dinner."

Chris Rider looked at him for a while, still bent over so she could see him through the window, her considerable breasts straining against her blue T-shirt.

She said, "We're not ready for that. You can buy me a drink."

The bar was darkly lit by little lamps hanging down from the ceiling. A marble bar with red-covered stools and a brass rail to rest your feet on. Behind the bar there was a painting of some French village with something French written underneath it. To the right of that, a flat-screen television with some guys from CNBC discussing the stock market.

Chris Rider sipped her vodka tonic and set it on the square red napkin on the bar. She said, "That's a straight Coke?"

"Yeah."

"Do you ever drink?"

"Rarely."

Chris tilted her head a little and said, "You have that in common with him. That and your taste for ugly cars."

Bridger said, "Seth didn't drink?"

"No. I mean, he'd order a whiskey or something, but just the one and he'd rarely finish that. He didn't seem to trust alcohol."

"His dad drank."

Chris said, "You mean your dad."

Bridger nodded.

"Was he a bad man?"

"More weak than bad."

"And you don't like weak people, do you? I think you have more sympathy for someone who's mean than someone who's weak."

"Do you?"

"Your brother wasn't weak. Not by any means."

Bridger let that pass. He said, "This is a nice place. Do you come here often?"

"Sometimes. It's owned by two brothers

from Lyon, France. I used to date one of them."

"The one who greeted us at the door?"

"No. The other one. He works in the kitchen. He'll probably come out here in a minute and say hello. I'll have to introduce you and he'll ask where you're from and you can tell him and then if he has time or if he's bored he'll ask you what you do and I'll be curious what you say then."

Bridger looked at her.

And she said, "Why didn't you tell me you had been in prison?"

"Should I have?"

"It's something you should tell a lady."

"It's something you should tell a parole officer. If you're under their supervision."

"How do you know you're not?"

"Did you check on me?"

"I did not," she said. "I was told."

"By your boss?"

Chris Rider snorted. "God, no. She wouldn't leave her Krispy Kremes to take the time. No. It was a co-worker. And a friend. He said you had done time for breaking and entering. But that's not all."

"He also told you that I was still active. Right?"

"Active . . . is that what you would call it? They say you killed some people in Pennsylvania. Is it true?"

"I wasn't charged."

"That's not what I asked you."

"They were trying to kill me. And a lady who had done nothing to harm anyone."

"Oh, so it wasn't a *selfish* murder? You were defending a damsel in distress. How noble of you."

"No, it wasn't just about her."

"That's what I thought. Just what do you have in mind, Mr. Bridger? You want me to help you find whoever killed Seth so that you can put them down? Restore honor to the family name?"

"That's not what I want."

"I don't believe you. Let me tell you what Seth would want. He would want, *maybe* he would want, the killer caught and arrested and tried and convicted. He would not want some vendetta carried out by a brother who didn't give a shit about him while he was still alive."

"How do you know? Maybe he'd appreciate the gesture."

"I knew him better than you."

After a moment, Bridger said, "Yeah, you probably did. But I still want to know what happened. The police don't seem very interested."

"Why do you think that?"

"I met with Detective Wilkening again. He seemed to take the same view of me as you. I think he was almost relieved to learn I was a crook."

"How do you figure that?"

"If the brother is dirty, maybe Seth was too. He figures that maybe deep down Seth had it coming. It helps him, you see. Now he doesn't have to feel bad about doing as little as possible."

"You're surmising."

"He said that something like half the homicides in this city go unsolved. Do you agree?"

"I'm not a homicide detective."

"I asked if you agree."

"I don't know. Maybe it's a slight exaggeration."

"Maybe. Maybe if it's black guys who wear red do-rags killing black guys who wear blue, they're not that interested in solving the murders. Less gangsters for them to worry about. But that's not what we're dealing with here. Seth was law enforcement. Usually they work very hard to catch someone who killed a cop."

Chris Rider looked ahead, not at Bridger. "Usually," she said softly.

Bridger said, "There's something else. He usually carried a notebook with him. A small notebook that fit into his jacket pocket. The police didn't find that notebook. It wasn't on him. What do you think of that?"

Chris said, "I don't know."

"You don't *know?*"

"Well, I guess it is unusual. Maybe he left it at home."

"He didn't. I checked. Is it at his office?"

"No. I mean, I don't think so."

"I cleaned out his desk. I didn't see it." Bridger looked at her for a moment. "Unless you took it," he said.

"Why the fuck would I take it?"

"I don't know. I'm just asking."

"Well, don't ask me things like that. Don't accuse me of things. I was his friend."

"Okay," Bridger said. "I got a list of his offenders."

Chris sighed. "I told you not to do that."

Bridger said, "It's a long list. Maybe you could go over it with me. Tell me which ones I should look into."

"I'm not doing that. One, I could lose my job. Two, it would be a waste of time anyway."

"Maybe you'll think about it."

"I won't," she said.

Bridger stood up and put money on the bar for their drinks.

"Maybe you will," he said.

Bridger walked down the city street to his car. It was dark outside. He saw a man walking toward him, a big man with his head down. Bridger looked at him then started to turn but then it was too late, the blackjack clipping him above the ear. It did not knock him unconscious but it hurt him and he slumped and the two men grabbed him and pushed him into an alley. They frisked him and took Seth's .38 snubnose out of his jacket pocket. Then they hit him with the blackjack again, this time in the kidneys and he stumbled and they kept going, almost carrying him and they went past a dumpster and pushed him down.

It was dark and the ground was wet. The big men who stood over him wore caps and Bridger could see they were black guys. Bridger started to get up and they took turns kicking him. He fell back, started to rise again and one of them swung the blackjack and smacked him across the face. Bridger fell to his left, knocking his head against the side of the dumpster. The attackers laughed.

Bridger wished he hadn't left the other guns in the car. He put his hands over his head, hoping to deflect a blow from the blackjack that could kill him. This led to more kicks. After a while it stopped and one of the men squatted down. The man wore black gloves. He grabbed Bridger's chin and pushed it back so that Bridger's head was pressed against the wall.

The man, whose name was Jim Patterson, said, "You like that?"

Bridger didn't answer.

Patterson said, "Because it can get a whole lot worse. A whole lot worse. You understand?"

Bridger said nothing. Patterson bonked his head against the wall.

"Understand?"

"Yeah, I understand."

"Good," Patterson said. "Now listen to me. America's a big country with many opportunities. We'll take Seattle and you can have the rest of it. Now that's a reasonable proposition, my friend. Wouldn't you say?"

Bridger didn't answer him. He was on the verge of losing consciousness.

Patterson said, "We got planes leaving this city everyday. Be on one of them tomorrow. 'Cause if I see you again, I'm going to kill you."

The other man, Hammond, said, "We'll be watching you."

124

Patterson pushed Bridger over and left him there.

# FOURTEEN

A black man in a white smock mopped spots off a floor. A trail of spots leading to a large blotch. Bridger took it in as best he could. It was a horizontal view. He turned his head and looked up. A ceiling. He was on his back, but not on the ground. Elevated. He realized he was on a gurney. Which meant he was in a hospital. He started to piece things together. In a hospital but not in a hospital room. He was on a gurney in the hall. He turned back to look at the black man mopping the floor. Blood. The man was mopping up blood. Was it his?

He became aware of people near him. Talking. A woman's voice and a man's. The female voice saying they were waiting for a neurosurgeon to look at the patient's head, make sure he hadn't suffered a subdural hematoma. They were talking about him.

Bridger said, "Hey." Hearing his own voice, it sounded weak and slow.

The male physician said, "Just a *minute.*" And that was all Bridger remembered for a while.

He woke up later in a hospital bed. On the television, Regis and Kelly pretending to squabble over something. Bridger knew he hadn't turned that on. He looked to his right and saw a guy sitting up in his bed. The guy looked over at Bridger and nodded and returned his attention to the set. Bridger nodded back and looked to his left. Light in the window. Morning.

Bridger asked the guy in the other bed how to get ahold of the nurse.

The guy said, "That button on your right. Yeah, that one."

Bridger pressed it. A few minutes later a pint-sized nurse came in. She was cute and petite and she didn't wear any makeup or perfume. She asked him some questions and he answered them and then she told him a doctor named Herron wanted to talk with him before he checked out.

Dr. Herron came in later and told him he was okay. Told him that they had done a CAT scan to make sure he didn't have a serious head injury and that Dr. Campbell, a neurosurgeon, had done an examination and cleared him.

Dr. Herron said, "We thought you would be okay, but we wanted to bring the neurosurgeon in just to make sure."

"That sounds expensive," Bridger said.

Dr. Herron frowned. "We had to be sure."

Bridger nodded. He now knew that this was the doctor who had been in the hallway the night before. The one who had told him, "Just a minute."

Dr. Herron said, "Your insurance will cover it."

Bridger had a ten-thousand-dollar deductible. But that wasn't this guy's fault. Bridger said, "Yeah. Thanks. Can I go?"

"Yeah. You're free to go." The doctor paused. "What happened?"

Bridger said, "Had an accident, I guess."

"Were you mugged?"

"No."

"Do you even remember what happened?"

Bridger didn't answer and the doctor said, "The run report said you were found by the street. A couple of people on a date saw you and called 911. They said you looked like you'd been assaulted. Which is a fair assessment, given the extent of your injuries. They thought maybe you'd crawled out of the alley and passed out."

Bridger said, "Nothing broken, though?"

"No, nothing broken, no permanent damage. Some contusions and you're going to feel those for a while. Have your personal physician prescribe some painkillers. Rest for a week, maybe two. What is it you do?"

"I'm an auto mechanic."

"Well, I wouldn't do any heavy lifting for a while. Whether or not you want to report the assault to the police is up to you. I think you should, but that's your decision."

"Thanks."

He dressed and checked out. He moved stiffly and slowly, aware of the bruises and discoloration to various parts of his body, the bandages covering cuts on his face. He looked and felt like a man who had gotten the shit kicked out of him by people who knew how to do it. Two black guys, the one doing the talking in a smooth, calm voice, telling him he'd better get out of town if he didn't want to die.

He took a cab back to the place where he had left the Chrysler. The Chrysler was still there but it had a parking ticket on it. Bridger looked at the car and then back at the mouth of the alley. He tried to remember crawling to the end of that alley to the street where people could see him and call an ambulance. He didn't remember that part. He remembered the men beating him but what happened after that was hazy.

What had he intended to do? Crawl to the car and drive away? What if he had made it to the car? Then what?

Bridger tossed the parking ticket in the street and got in the car and drove it back to his hotel. He parked in the hotel garage and opened the trunk. The box with the guns was still there. He took the box to his hotel room. He took the guns out of the box and loaded them and put them on the desk.

He got the list of Seth's offenders out of his pocket and unfolded it. He looked up Natoya Carter's number. He used the phone in the hotel room to call her.

She answered on the fourth ring.

"Don't hang up. It's Dan Bridger."

Natoya said, "I told you, I got nothing to say."

"One question. When Seth came to see you, did he have a little notebook on him? One that he wrote in?"

Silence.

Bridger said, "Did he or didn't he?"

"Yeah," she said. "He always had it with him."

"And he had it the last time you saw him?"

"Yes."

"Thanks," Bridger said and hung up.

Bridger went back to the list. He read the

arrest summary of one of the offenders. He read it again. Then he called a friend of his in Kansas City.

Thirty minutes later, he checked out of the hotel.

# FIFTEEN

The girls in the yellow shirts gained possession of the soccer ball and began charging down the field to the goal. A couple of defenders missed their tackles and parents on the sidelines began to cheer. The yellow team approached the goal and one of the girls took a shot and the ball went wide.

Dean Coates was assistant coach of the other team of girls. They wore red uniforms.

It was a nice Saturday morning. Blue skies and cool, crisp temperatures. Other teams played on other fields and other parents watched. The game continued for a few more minutes until a whistle blew. A 1–1 tie where everybody won and nobody lost. Coates talked with his wife and they told their little girl she played great. They talked with other parents. Coates's wife said they could use some pizza and Coates said he would join them later, really.

Mrs. Coates left, taking their daughter

with her. Dean walked to a picnic area under an open shelter with an outdoor grill. He saw a man there, leaning against a post, looking out on the fields.

Jim Patterson said, "Soccer is not an American sport."

Coates said, "What are you talking about? You see all those kids out there?"

"Yeah."

"What are they, Russians?"

Patterson turned to him. "What do you know about it? You coaching those kids, you never even played the game."

"I played a little, in college. I could have made the team, if I'd wanted."

Patterson kept his smile to himself. He was used to Dean's ego. Dean believed he could conquer any sport, but *chose* not to. There was no telling Dean he wasn't some kind of Bo Jackson. Patterson said, "Little girls play it on Saturdays until they get interested in boys. But it's never gonna catch on like football or basketball. Not in my lifetime."

Coates said, "How did it go?"

Patterson said, "We gave him a good country beating. Enough to put him in the hospital, but nothing broken that I know of."

"Enough . . . did he go to the hospital?"

"Yeah. Ambulance came and got him about a half hour after we did it. He left the hospital this morning, though."

"How do you know that?"

"Hammond's watching him. He's at his hotel now."

"Still?"

"He's got twenty-four hours. It's still morning."

"What did you think?"

Patterson said, "What do you mean, what do I think?"

"I mean, what do you think of him?"

Patterson said, "You ever been beat? I don't mean just hit or knocked down, but beaten bad."

Coates shrugged. He wasn't going to answer.

"I have," Patterson said. "When I was a kid. I'll tell you something, you don't forget something like that. It stays with you. You can't sleep, you hurt so bad. And you feel scared inside and ashamed too."

"Yeah?" Coates said. "I'll feel better when he leaves."

"We should have just done him."

"When I say so," Coates said.

Patterson said, "What if he doesn't leave?"

"Then we do it," Coates said. "You think he won't?"

Patterson looked back out to the fields. "I don't know," he said.

Coates said, "You just told me something about the psychological effects of being beaten. How you don't forget it."

"I did. But this man . . . well, I don't know. He didn't cry out. He didn't beg us to stop. He just took it. Like he was waiting for it to end. Like maybe he knew we wouldn't kill him. While it was going on, I didn't think much about it. But now I'm wondering if it was a mistake, letting him live."

"Bad karma?"

"A superstition, maybe. You know how our people are about superstitions."

"I think you're thinking too much about it," Coates said. "He's nothing, anyway. A thief. A burglar."

"And what are we?"

Coates smiled. "What you talking about, *what are we?* You think we're gangsters or something?"

Patterson shrugged.

"Man," Coates said, "now is not the time to start waxing philosophical. We are on the verge of something good. All of us. You deserve it. I deserve it. Our families deserve it. But if you have doubts, tell me now."

"I don't have doubts. I did what you told me."

"And I'm grateful to you, brother. Listen to me, a gangster is some piece of shit goes around wearing colors on his head, lives strictly for today, doesn't much care if he lives or dies. That's not us."

"No," Patterson said. "We're entrepreneurs."

There was a slight pause before they both started laughing, Patterson eventually saying he needed some sleep.

They parted on good terms and Coates walked back to his car.

On the drive to the pizza place, Coates thought about Jim Patterson. They had not grown up in the same neighborhoods, though they were roughly the same age. They had enrolled in the police academy the same year. They had endured the same racial slights and, through the years, maybe even fostered the same resentments. After two years in uniform, they had both been assigned to work undercover in narcotics. They were what was known as "field enforcement." This was a lot less glamorous than it sounded. There were no *Miami Vice* Ferrari Daytonas or designer clothes for them. They were there strictly to go after the low-level dealers peddling crack in shit-house ghettos. Buy-bust boys. They were put there because they could blend in and serve as cannon fodder in the pointless war on drugs. Officers like Coates and Patterson would pose as gang-bangers, negotiate drug buys. Make the deals, then the backup team would charge in and make the arrests. They played the roles of the street-hustling, hard-charging niggers, and they got good at it. If they didn't they'd get their throats slit. It was what Coates was taught to do, what he was told to do. His narcotics field officer once said, "It's not enough to act. You have to *become*. You have to be the person they want to see. Because if they find out you're a cop they'll lunch you." Dean Coates became.

One night he and Patterson were sitting in a car on a dark street when a black male appeared at the window and demanded to know what gang they were with. Dean told him to get his sorry ass out of there and the guy commenced to punching Dean in the face. Dean pulled his gun from his coat and shot the brother twice in the chest. They rushed out of the car to see the guy squirming on the ground like a fish and Dean shot him two more times in the head.

Patterson said, "Goddamn, Dean. What'd you do that for?"

"Nigger had it coming," Coates said.

But the guy wasn't armed and Coates had used his service weapon. They weren't sure if there were any witnesses. They decided it was best not to take any chances. So they stuck a throwdown weapon in the guy's hand and called their narcotics squad leader.

Jim Patterson would later tell the internal investigators that Dean Coates had saved his life that night. That Dean Coates was a hero. The internal investigators ruled that it was a clean shoot and Dean Coates was given a Medal of Valor for courage in the line of duty.

After that, Coates and Patterson requested a transfer out of narcotics. When asked why he sought the transfer, Coates answered, somewhat truthfully, that working narcotics had worn him out. That he was becoming stressed by the long hours and the paranoia of being found out by dealers and gangsters. What he did not say was that he feared retaliation from friends of the brother he had popped.

Coates worked uniform patrol for a while, but soon grew bored with it. He applied for the patrol lieutenant's position, but was rejected. He was told he had scored well on the written exam but had not impressed the board in his orals. Coates thought too many of the board members had something personal against him, maybe something against blacks in general. One of the board members had asked him if an officer could ever be the same after working undercover. Coates said, "In what respect?" Putting a little edge in his tone, which they didn't like apparently.

*Fuck 'em,* he thought. He didn't want to be a patrol lieutenant anyway. It was too limiting. After he was denied the promotion, Coates let it be known that he was considering legal action against the department for racial discrimination. He did this even though he knew he had no intention of filing an EEOC claim. In time he met with some members of the brass and told them his idea of starting a new police unit called Special Investigations Unit. Coates said the goal of the unit was to combat gang activity in the black community. In ways subtle and not so subtle, he let it be known that the creation of such a unit would persuade him to put aside any thoughts of pursuing legal action against the department. Fears of years of litigation and onerous enforcement decrees permeated the police commissioner's office.

Coates got his way. The Special Investigations Unit was created and he was put in charge of it. He handpicked the members of the unit. Patterson and Dupree, who had worked with him in narcotics. Eatherly, who he had gone to the academy with. Hammond, who he had known since childhood and had partnered with when he was on uniformed patrol. They were all about the same age. They were men like him. Corruptible, malevolent, resentful, and greedy. They shared a contempt for criminals as well as a confidence that they were smarter than other cops. They were players who knew how to work the system. To a man, they believed they were good police officers.

They were also loyal to Coates, who was a natural-born leader.

For his part, Coates had a self-awareness uncommon to most men. He knew he wasn't the smartest cop, but he believed he was smarter than most. He knew he wasn't the toughest cop (the toughest man he knew was Patterson), but he knew he was tougher than most. What he had over the others in his crew was an ability to lead and to make decisions and always remain cool. None of them had ever seen him unnerved, had never seen him panic.

Coates knew he was not popular among the older African American police officers. A good many of them seemed to sense he was bent. Though Coates persuaded himself they were just jealous of him. Coates had never felt much respect for them. To him, they were patsies. Kissing up to the man, hoping to nice-boy their way into promotions. In particular, Coates hated two black guys. One of them was Deputy Chief Carson Woods. The other was detective Charney Harris. Woods he hated because Woods had snubbed him like he was trash. Woods liked white people. Woods was an elmer. Harris was a different story.

# SIXTEEN

The bartender was a girl in her late twenties who wore a low-cut dress that was black at the top and purple and yellow striped at the bottom. She wore her natural blonde hair up. On the flat-screen television behind the bar the President talked some more about the war in Afghanistan.

The bartender asked Bridger if he would like a drink. Bridger said he'd like a Coke. She told him they had Pepsi and Bridger went with that.

The girl brought it to him and didn't seem to show him much interest beyond that. He was not her type. She made customer conversation with a well-dressed couple down the bar. The male customer told her they had just got back from the Italian Riviera. The bartender said that must have been beautiful.

The girl came back and asked Bridger if he'd like to see a menu. Bridger said no, thank you and then asked her if she was Sandra Welch.

The girl looked at him sharply. Let a few moments go by before she spoke.

She said, "How did you know that?"

"You were a client of my brother's. His name was Seth."

"So what? What do you — wait a minute. What do you mean, was?"

"He was killed. Didn't you know?"

"No. Oh God. What happened?"

"He was shot to death. Killed in a parking lot."

Bridger showed her his driver's license. "See," he said. "Same last name."

"My God. I was supposed to see him tomorrow. . . . No one told me."

She looked down at the customers at the bar. She looked back at Bridger. In a lowered voice, she said, "What do you want?"

"I want to know if you knew anything about his death."

"How would I know? I'm making a living here. This is a nice place. You — you don't know . . ."

"I know what you did. I don't care."

"I don't do it anymore. That's in the past."

"I told you, I don't care if you do or you don't. But the outfit you worked for, it was run by the mob. An offshoot of the

D'Angelo family in Kansas City."

"You know them?"

"I'm familiar with them."

"How would you know that? Your brother didn't even know that."

"My brother supervised you because you got busted running dope through the airport. Kansas City to Seattle. I know some people in Kansas City and I had a hunch you might know the same people. So I made a couple of calls."

Bridger waited. Now he had the young lady's attention.

Bridger said, "I know Frank D'Angelo."

She couldn't hide the alarm in her face. Scared now, she said, "Is he your friend?"

"No, he's not my friend. He's not anybody's friend. He's a piece of shit. He's also a psychotic murderer. Even his family has trouble keeping him under control. You were his girlfriend."

Sandra Welch said nothing. She was trying not to cry.

"Was," she said, her voice a whisper.

"Do you know about his past?"

"I heard."

"You know that three years ago, he had another girlfriend. She got involved with another man. And they both disappeared."

"I didn't know. I heard the rumor, like

everyone else."

"He's the jealous type."

"Yes, he was. You don't know the things he did to me. The feds leaned on me to turn him over. I didn't and I spent eighteen months in prison because of it. It was worth it not to die."

"Did he have anything to do with my brother's death?"

"No. I haven't seen or heard from Frank D'Angelo in years. He didn't kill your brother. And let me tell you something else. I had nothing going on with Seth. He never made a pass at me, never acted badly. He was kind. Unlike you."

"I don't think he knew what a dangerous piece of merchandise you were."

"No, he didn't. But I had nothing going on with him. If I had, Frank would've killed us both. No, wait. That's not what I mean. If I had and Frank still was watching me, he would've killed us both. I know that now."

"Frank's not watching you?"

"No. After I went to prison, he found another girl. God knows how long she'll make it."

Bridger looked at her for a while. He said, "Maybe prison was an escape."

"Maybe," she said. "Frank D'Angelo did not kill your brother."

"Because you're alive, huh? Apart from that, how are you so sure?"

"Because if he had, he would have told me. That's the kind of man he is. Now will you please leave me alone? Please."

The girl wiped tears from her eyes. Bridger put fifty dollars on the bar and left.

Bridger pulled the Chrysler out of the parallel spot on the street. He drove two blocks west and made a right turn. A block or two later he saw the green Jeep Cherokee in his rearview mirror. He had seen the Jeep before, shortly after he checked out of his hotel room. He believed the man behind the wheel was expecting him to drive to the airport. Bridger continued driving for another few blocks. Then he pulled into a multilevel parking garage. He stopped to pull the parking ticket and while he did that he looked in the rear mirror and saw the Jeep drive behind him. There was only the driver in the Jeep.

There were twelve levels in the garage. Bridger parked on the tenth, slipping the Chrysler into a space between a van and a Toyota. He opened the glove compartment and removed a pen and a receipt from a tire place. There was nothing else to write on. He got out of the car and quickly moved to the row of cars on the other side of the lot. He crouched behind a Chevy Suburban and waited.

About a minute passed, not much more, when the Jeep Cherokee came up the incline. The Jeep passed the Chrysler, stopped and then backed up. Bridger saw the number on the license plate and wrote it down on the receipt. He slipped the receipt into his pocket. He waited.

A black man got out of the Jeep and walked over to the Chrysler and looked inside. He saw nothing and he looked around the garage. Then he looked at the stairwell and the entrance to the elevator. He seemed to think about walking to the stairs. Then he thought better of it and got back in the Jeep.

The Jeep made the next turn and started downward, out of the garage.

Bridger ran to the Chrysler.

Hammond was pissed.

They had sent him to watch the man. Keep an eye on him, but not kill him. Dean had been specific about that. We'll give him a day, Dean had said. We're not animals. Give him a day to heal from his beatin' and if he doesn't leave town then we'll kill him and it'll be his fault. Hammond wondered if it made sense. They had put enough hurt on the man last night to send him to the hospital. The man had left the hospital this morning, so did that mean the clock started ticking then? Jim had told the man in no uncertain terms, be on a plane tomorrow. Now it was lunchtime and the man was parking his car in a goddamn garage downtown. Why? Why do that? Drive the car to the goddamn airport and get out of town. We said go, now go. All this Marshal Dillon shit — *I want you out of town by sundown* — give the man a warning and if he doesn't listen put a fucking cap in his head. Mean what you say.

But Dean had said not to kill him unless Dean gave the order. Dean said, *Just stay on the man, you hear?* That was typical Dean. He never trusted anyone in his crew to do things themselves, to use their own initiative. Hammond thought, *I should've just followed him directly into the garage and shot him.* Say to the man, "What are you still doing here?" Or, "You don't listen too good, do you?" Then shoot him in the face. Then get out of there. Or put a gun in his hand and claim self-defense. Officer performing his duty. That should fly. The man was a criminal, after all.

But no, he had let the man get a head start

on him. He had not expected the man to pull the car in a parking garage only a few blocks from where he had been. If he had pulled the Jeep in right behind the man, the man may have looked in the rearview mirror and recognized a guy who had beaten the shit out of him the night before. Never get too close in a surveillance. A rookie mistake.

And now what?

Now he would have to leave the garage and find a spot to park on the street and wait for the man to come back and get in his car and leave the garage. More waiting. Shit duty.

Hammond made the last turn and drove down the slope to the ticket booth. He stopped at the booth and handed the attendant his stub. The attendant said, "Ten dollars." Even though he had only been in there for a couple of minutes. Hammond sighed angrily and reached into his pocket.

He heard the sound of an engine accelerating and looked into the rearview mirror to see the green Chrysler hurtling down the ramp toward him. He didn't register it right away. His mind just thought, *no,* but the Chrysler didn't slow, it just kept coming, the engine getting louder.

The Chrysler smacked into the back of

the Jeep, punching it forward, the windshield cracking as it made contact with the lowered cross bar, breaking it off as the Jeep was knocked out of the garage and halfway into the street.

The Chrysler stayed on him, pushing the Jeep all the way out into the street. Hammond stepped on the brake and pushed it to the floor, yelling now and turning around in his seat, seeing the man in the Chrysler behind him, just for a moment, before the Ford SUV plowed into him.

Bridger got out of the Chrysler and ran to the passenger side of the Jeep. He opened the door and found the man slumped over in the seat. Bridger grabbed him by the back of his jacket and pulled him out. The man groaned. He had been roughed up by the impact but Bridger punched him hard in the kidneys and heard him groan again. Bridger reached into the man's jacket and found a pistol. He took it out and threw it on the ground.

A crowd started moving to the scene of the collision. The man behind the wheel of the Ford SUV got out and asked if anyone was hurt. Bridger didn't answer him. He dragged Hammond to the back of the Chrysler, opened the trunk and threw him in. He slammed the trunk shut and got in the car and drove away.

# SEVENTEEN

The freight train clanked north, moving slowly past the abandoned shelter, the cars rust red and dirty white. The Chrysler came from the opposite direction, its tires crunching through gravel, slowing then making a left turn over the tracks and into the shelter.

Bridger got out of the car and moved to the back. He opened the trunk and pulled Hammond out. Hammond got to his feet and lunged at him, but he was weakened by the collision and his efforts were slow and clumsy. Bridger stepped out of reach then stepped back in and punched him in the gut. Hammond doubled over and Bridger grabbed the scruff of his coat and threw him to the ground.

Hammond looked up at him.

Between hard breaths, Hammond said, "Boy, you in a lot of trouble."

Bridger smiled at him. "Am I?"

"Big trouble. You just assaulted an officer

of the law."

Bridger took the man in. About thirty years old. Slim and tough and athletic. But maybe not too bright.

Bridger said, "You're a cop?"

The man reached into his shirt front. Bridger pulled the .45 from his pocket and held it at his side.

"Careful," Bridger said.

Hammond slowed his movements. Slowly, he pulled a department badge out of his shirt. The badge was clipped to a chain around his neck.

Bridger said, "Throw it over here."

Hammond pulled it off his neck and tossed it to him. Bridger said, "Stay on the ground." He picked it up.

Bridger read it aloud. "Michael Hammond."

"Yeah."

Bridger put it in his pocket.

"Hey," Hammond said. "I need that."

"What for?" Hammond didn't answer and Bridger said, "Well, what's the story?"

Hammond was struck by the calmness of this man. He didn't seem rattled or upset by the fact that he had kidnapped a police officer. Hammond gave him the tough-cop look, the willful ignorant one he'd use with a defense lawyer in court. He said, "What

153

do you mean?"

"You and your rather large friend beat the shit out of me last night. How come?"

"I don't know what you're talking about."

"You said you'd be watching me. And you kept that promise."

"I think you're confused."

"Is your friend a cop too?"

"What friend?"

"The one that was with you last night."

"I'm sorry, but I thought I told you. I don't know what you're talking about." Hammond smiled. "It seems you've kidnapped the wrong man. A cop. Now that's bad luck."

"For you, yeah," Bridger said. "Well, I'll tell you something, Officer Hammond. I'm going to keep your identification and I'm going to let you go. You can tell your friend that I'm not leaving town. Maybe you and him can file charges against me. But I don't think you're going to do that, you crooked piece of shit. Because then you'll have to explain why it is you beat me up and threatened to kill me. And maybe then you'll have to explain what you had to do with killing my brother."

"Fuck your brother. And fuck you too."

Bridger raised the pistol and fired twice. Hammond cried out, pulling himself into a shell. The bullets ricocheted off the ground, where Bridger had aimed them. Hammond's hands over his head, Hammond screaming now, "Don't, *don't!* Please don't kill me!"

Bridger said, "I told you to be careful."

Bridger got into the Chrysler and left.

# EIGHTEEN

Coates said, "Yeah, but what did you tell him?"

"I told you," Hammond said. "I didn't tell him anything."

"But he said something about his brother. How did he know to say that to you?"

"Man, how should I know? The man guessed."

A Boeing 747 climbed the sky over them, starting its flight to Chicago. All of the crew was there — Eatherly leaning up against his car, Dupree and Patterson standing in the background.

Coates maintained his focus on Hammond. He asked, "But how would he guess something like that?"

"Dean, I told him nothing. Why won't you believe me?"

Coates said, "I'm just trying to get it straight, that's all."

"You told me to keep an eye on him. I did that."

"You let him take you," Patterson said.

"Was I talking to you?" Hammond said. "I don't believe I was talking to you."

"I'm talking to you," Patterson said.

Coates held up a hand to Patterson, telling him to calm down and that he would handle this. Coates said, "Why did he go into the garage?"

"I don't know."

Patterson snorted.

Coates said, "He was leading you, wouldn't you say?"

"Yeah, maybe."

"Maybe setting you up," Coates added.

"He got lucky," Hammond said. "Anyone can get lucky. Look, this is not my fault. I said we should have whacked him from the beginning. You're the one that said we should give him a warning."

Coates smiled. "So it's my fault?"

"I'm not saying that, Dean. I'm only saying that I shouldn't take the heat for all this."

"Okay, man," Coates said. "I made that call. And it was the right one. If any of you take issue with that, you can go your own way. That much less to split the take with. But if you still want in, you must always remember, this is my operation. Understand?"

"Yeah, Dean. I understand."

"Good." Coates seemed to relax. "Now you did good calling me first. Okay?"

"All right."

"Now tell me again what you told — who took the report?"

"Younger. Ken Younger. North Division."

"Oh, yeah. He's not too bright. That's good. So you told him you didn't know the man."

"Yeah."

Coates regarded Hammond for a moment, stretching it. Coates asked, "Why did you do that?"

"I thought it was best," Hammond said. "I thought it was what you would want me to do."

"You'd be right about that. But did you think it might be what he might want you to do, too?"

"I'm not afraid of him, if that's what you mean."

"No?"

"No. And something else: I had my reasons too. *I* don't want the department to know about him. Because the next time I see him, I'm going to kill him."

Coates looked from Patterson, smiled and

looked back to Hammond. Coates said, "Didn't you guys already tell him that?"

Hammond fumed silently over the insult. He didn't like being patronized, but he was deferential to Dean and a little scared of him too. But now Patterson felt like something was being said about him too.

Patterson said, "Like the man said, we did what you told us. You told us not to kill him. Now what are you telling us?"

Coates regarded Patterson, sensing the challenge. Coates asked, "What do you think?"

"I think I want to hear you say it," Patterson said.

"All right," Coates said. "I'm saying it. You find the man and you put him down. Permanently."

# NINETEEN

Elaine Ogilvie said, "I told you before, I have final exams."

"I know," Bridger said. "But isn't there some way to put that off?"

"You mean get an extension? No, there has to be an emergency of some sort. A death in the immediate family." Elaine hesitated. "Seth wouldn't count."

Bridger looked at her and said, "Even if you were having his child?"

They were in the cafeteria at the law school. A handful of students in there using the place to study, the students drinking coffee out of tall Styrofoam cups. One of them saying to another, "I have one night to learn a semester's worth of partnership tax. One night. I went to every class and I never understood what the fuck he was talking about."

Elaine Ogilvie looked back at Bridger. She asked, "How did you know about that? Did

Seth tell you?"

"No. I told you, we didn't talk. A co-worker told me."

"He told people at work?"

"He told one person, I think. She's okay. She's not going to tell everyone."

"She told you." Anger in her expression now. "It's private," she said. "Can't you understand that it's private?" Her eyes began to fill.

Bridger did not put a hand on her. He let her be with her thoughts, but stayed where he was. Finally, he said, "It's going to be okay."

"No, it's not," she said.

Bridger said, "What are you going to do?"

"I don't know," Elaine said. "My parents don't know yet. I'm going to have to tell them sooner or later. I'm not — I'm not going to have an abortion. Is that what you were asking me?"

"I don't think it's my business."

"It sort of is," she said. "Or maybe it isn't. I don't know. What are you doing here anyway?"

Bridger didn't answer her at first.

She asked, "Are you going to tell me he would want me to have it? That it's what he would have wanted?"

"I don't know what he would have wanted.

He told his friend at work that he was happy about it."

"He did?"

"Yeah."

The tears rolled down her cheeks. "Well," she said. "What do you know about that?"

"Did he tell you something different?"

"No. He told me that too. But you never know, do you? If they're telling you the truth or just telling you what you want to hear. Do you have any children?"

"No."

She smiled through her sadness and said, "No? And there was just you and him, right? So I'm it. It's left to me to carry on the Bridger name."

"I guess it is."

A heavy guy with curly black hair and glasses and an anxious expression walked over to a couple of students and asked if they'd seen his study group. He didn't name any names. One of the students looked at him blankly and the other suggested he check the library. The heavy guy sighed impatiently and walked off, like they had been unreasonable with him.

Elaine said, "Why do you want me to go to my parents?"

Bridger said, "I think Seth may have known about something . . . bad. I don't think he was killed randomly. Did he talk to you about his work?"

"Only in general terms. Nothing specific. He was a parole officer, not a detective. What could he have known?"

"I don't know. I'm trying to find out. He never said anything to you about corrupt police officers?"

"Never. What have you found out?"

"I don't want to go far into it. Maybe it's better for you not to know too much."

"So you'll tell me to leave town, but you won't tell me why."

"I don't have a reason to think you're in danger. But I have a bad feeling. And sometimes that's enough."

"Not for me." She regarded the bruise on his face, the cut above his eye. "I asked you before what happened and you didn't tell me."

"Didn't tell you what?"

"If you'd been beaten up."

"It's nothing."

"It doesn't look like nothing. It looks as if you've been in a fight. And if it's nothing, why are you telling me to leave town?"

"I'm not telling you anything. I'm asking you to consider it."

Elaine Ogilvie shook her head. "I don't like this. I don't like any of it. I don't like being told what to do. Not by anyone. And especially not by a criminal who's hiding things. But that's not all. Your brother got to a place in his life where he didn't care whether or not he knew you anymore. It took him a while to come to terms with the fact that his family didn't give a damn about him. It took him a while but he got there. He matured, you see. He accepted things as they were and he put it behind him. And now that you're here, I can understand why he did that. You come to town and within a couple of days you're in trouble with the police, getting in fights and you have the balls to try to tell me I should leave. You're a bad egg, Mr. Bridger. You're bad luck, and I want nothing to do with you anymore."

# TWENTY

An unmarked white Ford sedan pulled into the parking lot of a small shopping area. The strip contained a pizza delivery place, an animal feed store, an Ace Hardware shop and a drugstore that sold magazines and used paperback books. A guy got out of the Ford and walked into the drugstore.

He was a big man. White with black hair and long sideburns and a thick mustache. He wore heavy work boots and jeans and a blue shirt with a tie loosely knotted around his neck. His sport coat was a little tight on him. When he walked you could see the holstered gun on his belt. The man's name was Mitch Carnahan.

In the drugstore he walked past the magazine rack to the lunch counter at the back. Sitting on one of the red stools was a black guy in his mid-forties. He was short for a police officer, about five eight, bull shouldered and thick necked. He sipped from a cup of coffee. On a dish in front of him were a couple of slices of buttered toast.

Mitch Carnahan sat one stool away from him.

The black man, whose name was Charney Harris, said, "The coffee's good."

"Yeah?" Carnahan said. "I was hoping to get some breakfast."

Harris said, "It's after two. They don't serve breakfast after two. There's a lunch special. Chicken dumplings. It's good."

"Did you have it?"

"Not today. But I've had it here before. Just order that."

Carnahan told the lady behind the counter he'd have the special and a large iced tea. The lady ladled the dumplings into a Styrofoam bowl and set it on a Styrofoam plate. She slathered a butter-like substance on two white pieces of bread and put that on the plate next to the bowl. She placed the dish in front of him with a set of plastic utensils wrapped in a white napkin. Carnahan made a *hmmm* sound and told her it looked good. The lady said it was.

Carnahan slurped a couple of plastic spoonfuls. He said, "You know how hard it is to find food like this in the city anymore? I went downtown with the wife last Saturday, took my daughter and her boyfriend with us to some Chinese place I'd never been to. My daughter wanted to go there, impress this douchebag she met at college. We walk in and the maitre d' is wearing a suit like you'd see on a lawyer and right away I thought, oh no. I tried to find egg rolls on the menu and couldn't do it. Guess how much the tab was?"

"Hundred dollars."

"Two sixty. For the four of us. And we didn't even order wine."

Charney Harris said, "Downtown's not for hillbillies. The boy offer to chip in?"

"You fucking kidding? That little shit didn't have two nickels to rub together. Sophomore in college and of course, you know, he knows everything. I'm paying for his meal and he's got the ass to start lecturing me on something called 'community policing'? Seems he spent a semester in Spain. Or was it France? Wherever it was, he made a point of letting me know how much more 'progressive' the European police are than the American cops."

Harris smiled. "He said that to you? When you were paying for his meal?"

"Oh, yeah."

"I'm beginning to like this guy."

"Let him date your daughter then."

"Oh, no, no. I don't approve of interracial dating."

Carnahan nodded sagaciously. "I know what you mean. You start mixing that blood and you get black presidents who dance like white men. Causes a lot of identity issues."

"He's black, man. I don't care how he dances. We acquired him in the racial draft. First round."

"Yeah," Carnahan said. "But we still got Tiger Woods."

"Keep him," Harris said. "Listen, you heard about Hammond?"

"I figured that's why you called me," Carnahan said. "He was abducted, apparently?"

"Yeah," Harris said. "I got a copy of the report."

"Who took the report?"

"Ken Younger. You know him?"

"I met him once," Carnahan said. "He did not blow me away with his intelligence."

"My feelings too. Hammond told him a whole lot of shit and he believed every word of it."

"How does a former homicide detective who's been exiled to the property room get a hold of such a report?"

"I still have some friends," Harris said. "Even in homicide. Witnesses say Hammond was in a vehicular collision and then

168

was placed into the trunk of a car and taken away. Hammond gets away and calls it in and tells Younger he barely got a look at the guy."

"A look at the guy who kidnapped him?"

"Yeah," Harris said. "Now what kind of shit is that?"

"You think he knew the guy."

"I'm sure he knew. Hammond is one of Coates's crew."

For a moment, neither of them spoke. Then Carnahan said, "Charney, I don't know."

"Hear me out," Harris said. "We both know Dean Coates is dirty. Hammond is one of his boys. There's no way that abduction was random."

"Okay, maybe it wasn't."

*"Maybe?"*

"Okay, *probably* it wasn't random. Probably Hammond knew his abductor. But how do we prove that?"

"If there was an internal investigation, something more than just a traffic report."

"There isn't," Carnahan said. "Someone has to file a complaint for that."

"I could file the complaint," Harris said.

"You didn't witness anything," Carnahan said. "It doesn't involve you."

"It involves Coates."

169

"Yeah, and there's the problem. You filed a complaint against him before and he was cleared."

"He got lucky."

"And you didn't. You got transferred to watching paint dry in property. Charney, there were people in the department who wanted you terminated for filing a false complaint."

"It wasn't false."

"I know that. You know that. And Coates knows it too. But look at what you're up against. You've got a gang of African American cops who are probably stealing money from drug dealers. But you don't have any evidence to prove it. We got no witnesses, no tape. Nothing. You file a complaint now and they'll accuse you of wanting to settle a personal score."

"But I'm right."

"You are right. But even if the Commissioner believed you, he'd still squelch your complaint. Do you have any idea what the political consequences would be of going after a group of rogue cops all of whom are black? Do you know what that could do to the department? To the city? Well, the Commissioner does. And he's not going to fuck with it."

"And what about if he doesn't? Every

170

black cop in this department suffers because of this. We got five crooked black guys and half the department knows it. So the rest of us brothers are crooked niggers by association."

"Nobody thinks that."

"You don't know, Mitch. You can't know."

"All right," Carnahan said. "I can't know what it's like to be black. I know that, okay? But put that aside and think about yourself. You've got nineteen years in. You're, what, ten months from getting your twenty in. Do the ten months and retire and forget this fucking shit."

"Dean Coates is dirty. He's got to go down."

"You want to bring him down, okay. But people will say you're after him because you're jealous. He's a star and who are you? A middle-aged cop who got pushed out of homicide. Embittered and old."

"You think that?"

"Ah fuck you, Charney. You know what I think."

"Yeah, I know what you think. Sorry."

"I was best man at your wedding."

"I know. I'm sorry."

"Forget it," Carnahan said. He paused. Then he said, "Look, I hate the son of a bitch too. And I'll admit something to you.

I'm a little afraid of him myself."

"You're not afraid of anyone."

Carnahan said, "I'm not afraid of Coates physically. Put me in a room with him and I'll tear his fucking head off. But I am afraid of what he can do to me professionally. He knows how to work the system, and he is a mean son of a bitch. If he finds out I'm thinking of building a case against him, he'll file a complaint against me for discrimination."

"You're no racist."

"You think that matters to Coates? He'll make shit up and try to get me terminated. I hate the man but I'm not willing to end my career for him."

"I won't ask you to," Harris said. "I just want a little inside help. Okay?"

"Have you forgotten that they exiled me too? They've got me working plainclothes felony."

"I know. But you're closer to the circle than me."

Mitch Carnahan said, "I'll do what I can, brother."

# TWENTY-ONE

Bridger left the Chrysler in a parking lot downtown. The ticket attendant did not notice that the front of the car was smashed in or that both of the headlights were busted. The parking lot attendant just handed him the ticket and told him to put it on the dash on the driver's-side corner.

Bridger took a cab to the airport and rented another car. This time he got a blue Ford Crown Victoria. He missed the Chrysler. He had a feeling that the car had meant something to his brother and he regretted that he had damaged it. But he had been angry at that fucking cop, angry enough to want to kill him. It was not like Bridger to get like that. His business was not for hotheads. He knew something about vengeance, knew what it could do to a man, knew what it could take from him. The men who had busted him up had been cops. Maybe they were just off duty, working as hired muscle like anyone else. Maybe he shouldn't have taken it so personally. Maybe they had just been hired to beat him up and tell him to leave town and they didn't know why or want to know why. Maybe that's what it was. But then the cop had said to him, fuck your brother and Bridger had almost killed him. It had angered him more than the beating.

He had done some jobs once in a big city that was known for its corrupt police department. In that city, professional thieves were supposed to pay tributes to the local police. Make things smooth and easy. But Bridger had never played that game. It was bad enough to have partners in crime. To have those partners be law enforcement was to ask for trouble. It was like working with the Mob, maybe worse.

As he drove back into the city, it occurred to him that no one really wanted him here. His brother's girlfriend, the police, the good-looking probation and parole officer . . . no one wanted him. Elaine had good cause to be wary of him. To her, he was a thief. Trouble. Perhaps in some way she felt that he had been a curse to Seth. That his background had maybe doomed Seth too. Maybe the girl was right. But he believed Seth would not have agreed with her. But he respected the girl for telling him to beat it, maybe even admired her for it. She reminded him a little of the lady he knew in Philadelphia. A nice girl who was tough and smart and knew what she was about. One of the nice girls who were off limits to him because of the life he had chosen. But Seth had been good enough for her.

Seth. What would Seth want? Would he, too, tell Bridger to get out of town? Bridger could tell himself that. But he wouldn't believe it. He couldn't abandon him twice.

Chris Rider parked in the driveway of her modest three-bedroom house. She unlocked the front door and let herself in. She put her keys on a table by the sofa. She hung her coat in the closet and stood in the living room. She stopped and turned her head. She pulled her .38 snub revolver from her holster and moved into her bedroom. She pointed the revolver at Bridger's back.

He was sitting at her desk in her bedroom, looking at her computer.

Chris said, "Put your hands on your head and turn around."

Bridger raised his arms and swiveled around in the chair.

Chris said, "How the hell did you get in here?"

"It was pretty easy," Bridger said. "You ought to buy an alarm."

"I ought to shoot you now," she said. "Claim self-defense."

"Maybe you should. Or you could call the police."

"I intend to."

Bridger said, "Did you call them the other night?"

Chris frowned. "What are you talking about?"

"The last time I saw you," Bridger said. "I walked out and a couple of cops accosted me. They weren't wearing uniforms. They roughed me up pretty good. Told me I had to leave town."

"I don't know anything about it."

"You sure?"

"Yeah." She lowered the gun a little. Unsure of herself now. She raised it again. "Look, I can see you got beat up. But that doesn't excuse you breaking into my home. Keep your hands up."

"I am. You didn't call those guys?"

"I told you, I don't know anything about it."

"Do you know a police officer named Michael Hammond?"

"No."

"If you did set me up, I'll find out about

176

it eventually."

"I didn't."

"But if you did, I'll find out. So if you did, you should probably go ahead and kill me now."

"I did not set you up. Now stand up and come out of there."

She motioned him out of her bedroom and into the kitchen. She kept the gun pointed at him and nodded for him to sit at the kitchen table.

Bridger said, "Are you going to call 911?"

"Shut up," she said. "What were you doing in my bedroom?"

"I wanted to see if you kept files on your offenders."

"I don't in my home, okay? You had no business going through my personal things."

"I just looked at your computer."

"It's private, damn you. You had no business going through it."

"I'm sorry. Really."

She still had the gun pointed at his chest. He said he was sorry and she believed him. Believed a criminal. She didn't know what to do. She couldn't shoot him. He was Seth's brother. She couldn't call the cops on him. Couldn't call the cops on a thief.

She holstered her weapon.

"If you wanted my help, you should have

called me. Don't break into my home, ever. It's a violation."

"I'm sorry. But I needed to be sure that you weren't in on it."

"In on what?"

"I was afraid you had set me up. I had to be sure you weren't part of it."

"Are you sure now?"

"I think so."

She didn't say anything, just looked at him with something between fury and disappointment.

Bridger said, "I didn't look at anything personal."

"You didn't look at my Facebook account?"

"No."

"Because my children look at that. My family —"

"I didn't look."

She gave him another look. Finally she said, "I'm not comfortable having you in my home. Do you understand that?"

"I do. I'll leave."

"I'll talk to you," she said. "But not here. Not in my home."

A few moments passed, the cute lady parole officer looking at the thief at her kitchen table. Then Bridger said, "How about I buy you dinner?"

■ ■ ■ ■

Chris said, "I still don't think you trust me."

They were at a quasi-rustic restaurant sitting in a booth with high wooden backs. They had some privacy. The salad was in little unstylish bowls that held little more than a fistful of lettuce and vague shavings of carrots. The waitresses called them hon and brought them meat dishes with large baked potatoes loaded with sour cream and cheese.

Bridger said, "You like places like this, huh?"

"I don't care to be seen with you," Chris said. "You abducted a police officer."

"I told you before. He was one of the guys that beat me up and threatened to kill me."

"Why would he do that?"

"He wouldn't tell me."

"I don't blame him," Chris said. "You still haven't answered my question."

"What question?"

"I asked if you trusted me."

"You said I didn't trust you."

"Whatever. I told you before, I don't know this —"

"Hammond."

"I don't know him. Did you bring me here

to see if they would follow? To use me to draw them out?"

"I thought of that."

"So . . . what do I do? Wait for you to go to the bathroom, then call them and have them come here?"

"You can do that now."

"Maybe I will."

They were quiet for a time. Then she said, "I can check on Hammond if you like. See what I can find out."

Bridger said, "Did Seth work with police officers?"

"No more than the rest of us. I told you before, cops sort of look down on probation and parole officers."

"Does that bother you?"

"Sometimes. It didn't bother Seth though."

Bridger said, "I went through Seth's list of offenders. I checked on one of them. Sandy Welch. You know her?"

"No. Why did you check on her?"

"She was involved with a gangster I'm familiar with. I thought there might have been a connection."

"Did you talk to her?"

"Yeah. A little."

"You shouldn't have done that."

"Well, I did. But there wasn't anything there."

"She could file a complaint, you know."

"Against who?"

Chris Rider didn't have an answer for that. She said, "Well, he had about sixty offenders under his supervision. That's one you've crossed off the list. What about the rest?"

"I was thinking that myself. I took a shot and it didn't work out. To tell you the truth, I was getting close to giving up on the whole thing. Even before I talked with the girl, I had a feeling it was a waste of time. I figured I was doing it for Seth, but then I wondered if I was doing it just to do it. Just to do something. Like I owed Seth at least the appearance of effort. But that's no good. No help to anyone. After that, I was considering hanging it up. Going to the airport and putting this rainy fucking city behind me. I sure as hell didn't want to get beat up again. Or killed. I told myself, maybe Seth *was* just killed by a cranked-out punk. And then I realized this cop was following me, the same one who had beat the shit out of me, and I changed my mind. I thought if this guy was willing to take the time to follow me, maybe even kill me, maybe there's something more to this."

"Sounds like you're grateful to this Hammond."

"In a way." Bridger said, "It's funny how people can help you see things."

Chris looked at him for a moment. "Yeah, funny."

Bridger looked back at her and said, "You're right, I don't trust you. Something's going on here that involves crooked cops. You say you're something less than a cop, but for me you're still law enforcement."

"I told you I don't know those men."

"You did."

"And I think you believe me. You know what else I think?"

"What?"

"I think you're trying to guilt me into helping you. You tell me you don't trust me so I'll want to prove you're wrong about me."

"Guilt you?"

"Manipulate. That's a better word."

"I'm a thief. Not a con man."

"A crook. And if there's one thing I learned, all crooks lie. Nothing is ever their fault."

"Seth wasn't a crook. I think Michael Hammond is. You have the ability to find out something more about Hammond, if you want." Bridger hesitated. Then said,

182

"I'll pay you for it. The way I would a private detective."

Chris said, "I don't want your money."

They were quiet during the drive back to the house. Bridger had the window cracked. Cool, moist air seeped into the car. Chris looked out the window, keeping her thoughts to herself.

When they got to her house, she turned to him.

She said, "I'm going to look into it. Okay."

"Okay," Bridger said.

"Not for you," she said. "I want you to understand it's not for you."

"I understand."

Chris said, "I'm going to explain."

"You don't have to."

"I'm going to, so shut up for a minute, okay? After you asked me about his missing notebook, I checked his desk. I checked all over the office. I couldn't find it. Now it's possible he lost it. It's possible it's at his apartment and you and his girlfriend haven't looked hard enough."

"We did."

She went on as if he hadn't said anything. "But I called the detective too. I called Wilkening and asked him about it. He wasn't happy to hear from me. In fact, he got a little shitty with me. Asked me what my name was again, even though I'd told him twice. That sort of shitty. I asked him if he'd found Seth's notebook in his state vehicle. He said no they hadn't. I didn't think he'd even looked. He seemed to sense that I thought that and told me I was welcome to look at it myself."

"Where is the vehicle?"

"It's back with probation and parole. I checked it."

"And?"

"And it wasn't in there."

"How long has your office had it back?"

"A day or two."

"And people have access to it?"

"Yes, people have access to it. But . . . that's not the point. The point is, it doesn't feel right. I see now where you were coming from. That Wilkening . . ."

"Now you understand."

"No, I don't understand. I don't understand you at all and I don't want to. Don't think I'm on your side because I'm not. Even though I'm going to help you."

"Can I call you tomorrow?"

"No. Do not call me at work. I'll call you."

"I don't have a cell phone."

"Get one. Then call me on my cell phone from a phone booth and tell me what it is."

"All right."

Chris opened the car door.

"One more thing," she said. "Next time you come to my house, you knock on the front door and ask if you can come in. If you come in any other way, I'll blow your head off."

# TWENTY-TWO

Tulie sat naked in the corner of her bedroom, crying. Dean Coates stood in the bathrobe that he kept at her place, trying to talk sense to the woman. But she kept crying and wouldn't listen. Sometimes it was hard to get her to listen. He didn't think she would get a black eye — he hadn't really hit her. Not with a closed fist. He had just pressed his hand against her face and pushed it with enough force that she fell off the bed. An accident. Now he was telling her to calm down when his cell phone rang.

"Baby," he said, "just be quiet for a minute, will you?"

He answered the phone.

"Yeah."

"Hey, man. You got time to talk?"

"If you got something good to tell me," Coates said.

Ramos didn't answer him at first, listening to the sound of the mistress wailing in the

186

background. Ramos said, "Man, you sound like you got problems." Smart assing him.

"Shut the fuck up," Coates said.

Ramos said, "Did I call at a bad time? Maybe I call back later."

"What have you got?"

Ramos said, "I think we in business. Can you meet me?"

"Yeah. In a half hour."

Driving away Coates felt better. He believed he had gotten Tulie to calm down. Talked her into getting back into bed, got dressed and went and got her a glass of water. Caressed her cheek with the back of his fingers, told her she was beautiful and that she knew he loved her. In time she accepted this and held the sheet above her breasts and stuck out her lower lip and asked him if he really had to be going so soon. Coates smiled at her and said he did.

He hadn't meant to knock her to the floor. But she had asked for it. She had done something nice for him, something he wasn't used to having so good and when she was finished, she had said, "I bet your wife can't do that. Not like that."

That's when he had told her to watch her fucking mouth, disrespecting the mother of his children. She told him she could say

187

whatever the fuck she wanted and then they started arguing and soon he covered her face with his hand and shoved her off the bed. He felt a certain satisfaction upon hearing her hit the floor.

Okay, she could have broken an arm or something in the fall. But she hadn't. Maybe got a bruise on her little ass, but she was okay. Goddamn, she had yelled though. Shouting and crying, calling him names. What if one of the neighbors had called the police? He would have been able to talk the cops out of doing anything — just a little disagreement, fellas — but they would have known him and they would have remembered her. And he didn't need that shit. He needed to keep things quiet. Particularly now.

Coates drove the car off the interstate exit ramp. He made a few turns and then he was under the highway that was dark among the concrete columns supporting the roads. He parked the car and walked about fifty yards until he came to a blue long-bed Ford pickup with white stripes and mag wheels.

Eddie Ramos got out of the truck and leaned against it with his hands in his pockets. He was a very thin man with wet brown eyes and patchy facial hair.

Ramos smiled at him and said, "I didn't

disturb you, did I?"

"Cut the shit," Coates said. "Did you talk to Ernesto or not?"

"Heyyyy," Ramos said. "What's with the attitude? I thought we were friends."

"Do I have a deal with the short man or not?"

Ramos shook his head, "Man, you better not call him that. Only the feds call him that."

"I'm doing business with him."

"That don't mean you're equals. Even I don't call him that. People don't show Mister Aguilar respect, he cuts off their fingers."

"In Mexico," Coates said. "Not on an American cop. Even he's not that bold."

Ramos smiled again. "Hey, what are we arguing for? We can do a deal. Just be respectful, huh?"

Coates said, "What's he offering?"

"We can give you five dollars a tab."

Coates laughed. "Five? Are you kidding? I can get a hundred on the street."

"Yeah. If you got the network to sell it. What are you going to do, have police officers deal it from their patrol cars?"

"I can find another buyer."

"Not with that much. You got what, two hundred fifty thousand?"

"Three hundred thousand."

"How are you going to unload three hundred thousand tabs?"

"I'll find another buyer. It's a free market."

"What do you want?"

"I'm reasonable," Coates said. "I can let it go for twenty a tab."

"That's six million dollars."

"Lunch money for Aguilar."

"But a lot of money for an underpaid cop. And his friends. We'll give you seven and half."

Coates shook his head. "You're not getting it. Why don't you go home, call Ernesto, have him come up here and I'll talk to him."

"Ernesto's not coming until the deal is set."

"How do I know you're authorized to offer anything? You could be selling me a line of shit."

"I'm authorized, believe that."

"Then stop dicking me around. I worked narcotics for three years, I know what this shit goes for. You take it to L.A., sell it for a hundred, maybe even a hundred twenty a pop. That's thirty million dollars."

"I know who you are, where you came from. Selling crack to homeboys on street corners don't make you no expert. You got about as much experience selling ecs as my sister. In L.A. it's going for fifty a pop."

"Bullshit. I'll go eighteen."

"Take it to Canada then," Ramos said. "See how well you do there."

Ramos started to get back in his truck. Coates's hand flicked to his sidearm. Ramos turned and looked at him.

Ramos smiled at him again. He said, "Man, what are you thinking?"

"Sorry," Coates said, moving his hand away from his gun.

Ramos said, "After all this, you're thinking that."

"Man, I said I was sorry. I didn't mean anything."

"I come here in good faith," Ramos said.

"I know that. Didn't I do something for you?"

Ramos said, "You didn't do that for me."

"All right," Coates said. "But I did it. You didn't have to go back to prison. It should mean something to you."

A few moments passed. Then Ramos said, "I tell you now, Ernesto's top figure is ten. I swear to you."

Coates said, "Ten dollars a tab?"

"If it's good," Ramos said.

"It's good. You have my word."

"More than that if it's not," Ramos said. "Three million then. Day after tomorrow.

I'll call you."

"Okay," Coates said.

From the cab of his truck, Ramos said, "Say hello to your lady for me."

# TWENTY-THREE

The district supervisor reassigned Seth Bridger's cases to the other parole officers. There was no meeting. It was done by memorandum. Each probation and parole officer picked up approximately ten more offenders. One officer asked if they were going to hire a replacement for Seth or were they just expected to work overtime to get the work done. The officer was told to show a little more sensitivity, as if he had something against Seth.

Chris Rider griped about it like everyone else. They were arguably understaffed even when Seth was still around. Those who complained too loud about the work conditions were liable to have their files audited for deficiencies that previously had gone unnoticed and were usually fabricated. Chris had a friend who had once put in eight hours overtime for work that legitimately needed to be done. The friend was disci-

plined for "unauthorized use of overtime"
and docked the very eight hours he was
owed. A thoroughly chickenshit, dishonest
way of avoiding compliance with state and
federal labor regulations. They had ways of
keeping the parole officers in line.

She discussed it with Marlon Gage in the
break room. Marlon put a dollar in the
vending machine for a moon pie while Chris
poured a cup of coffee over powdered
cream. Gage saying it wasn't right, the way
they treated their own people. Using Seth's
death to try to guilt them into submission.

Chris said, "I guess I shouldn't complain.
They only gave me nine."

"I got eleven," Gage said.

"Eleven? That's not fair," Chris said. "You
want me to take one?"

"No, I got it covered. How you holding
up?"

"I'm all right."

Marlon Gage said, "You heard from him
lately?"

"Who?"

"His brother."

Chris hesitated. She had never had anything against Marlon, but she had never
exactly confided in him either. She didn't
feel comfortable lying to him. Should she
now?

She said, "Not lately. He was here before, you remember."

"Yeah. I remember. I told you about him, you know."

"Yeah, you told me."

"He's got a criminal record."

"I know. You told me."

"And worse. I don't like to think what he's capable of."

"I remember what you told me," she said, her tone a little short. She paused. Then said, "Sorry. I know you mean well."

"It's okay," Gage said. "Do you know if he's still in town?"

Chris hesitated again. "I presume he is."

"Do you know where? He checked out of his hotel."

Chris looked at Marlon for a few moments. She said, "How did you know that?"

"I called and checked."

"How come?"

"I don't know. I just thought I should."

Chris asked, "Are you worried about him?"

"A little, yeah. I think he's dangerous."

"To who?"

"To you. Sorry, I know it's none of my business. But I got the feeling he's taking a liking to you. Or maybe something worse."

"What do you mean, worse?"

"Like maybe he wants to use you to get some information."

"Maybe. But maybe he just wants to find out what happened to his brother."

Marlon Gage gazed at her in a way she did not like. He said, "Why?"

"Why?" Chris said. "It's his brother."

"Okay, it's his brother. But were they that tight?"

"I don't think that's relevant."

"Isn't it? I never heard Seth say anything about him. Maybe Seth wrote him off for a good reason. The best people can have bad kin."

"You met him for what, two minutes?"

"He's bad news. I can tell that. And like I told you before, he's got a violent past. Who knows what he's been doing since he got here?"

Chris said, "You making a statement or are you asking me a question?"

"I'm talking to you as a friend," Gage said. "He'd be well advised to leave town."

For a while, neither of them said anything. Then Chris said, "I'm inclined to agree with you."

She finished her first client visit a little after ten o'clock in the morning. A guy who was on probation for KCSP — knowing concealment of stolen property. He was dressed in the uniform of a local fast-food restaurant. She would call his manager later to make sure he wasn't playing her. If he was, she wouldn't be hurt by it. It was a job where you got used to people lying to you and you didn't take it personally.

It had not been an easy life for Chris Rider. She got pregnant with her first child two months after her eighteenth birthday. She married the father of her child and they spent the next two years together. Her husband was still a child himself and in two years she came to understand he would never grow up. Her parents helped out with the baby and Chris worked full time as a receptionist in a law office. Middle-aged lawyers who were pudgy and lonely regularly made passes at her, which she found ways to reject while keeping her job. Meanwhile, her husband stayed at home and sat on his ass. It was not uncommon for her to come home from work, exhausted and her spirits low, and Bobby would ask her what she was going to make for dinner. A couple of years of that and she drafted her own divorce petition and got one of her bosses to sign it. Thus ended her first marriage.

She married for the second time when she was twenty-two, about a year before she started working as a parole officer. At twenty-three she had her second child. Her second husband was a cop who was about fifteen years older than her. His name was Brian. She was his second wife. He was a tall man with long sideburns and he looked good in his motorcycle boots and police helmet. A traffic officer who loved his bike and his work. One day he came home early from work and told her he was on paid suspension pending an internal investigation. She asked him what he was being investigated for and he told her insubordination. Later she found out from co-workers that he was being investigated for getting a blowjob from a prostitute while on duty and that the entire Seattle Police Department knew about it. When she confronted him about it, he cried and told her he was sorry for not being straight with her but he didn't want to lose her, especially now. She knew the weeping was a con job but she halfway fell for it anyway. She refused his request to appear at his side at the disciplinary hearing — show the disciplinary panel his wife was "standing by him." His union lawyer went with the sympathy strategy: client mans up, confesses to the misconduct and says he's sorry and no excuse and the lawyer argues that the officer was stressed from the daily horrors of police work, etc., and urges the disciplinary panel not to give the death penalty to the man's law enforcement career. The panel gave him sixty days without pay and a demotion. Chris stayed with him. A year later he got busted doing pretty much the same thing with a cashier at a convenience store while on duty. He lost his job that time and Chris divorced him.

Neither husband was much help with her kids. Apart from the few years she had with Brian, she had to raise them on her own. She struggled and she saved money and now her kids were both in college. She had avoided marriage after divorcing Brian. Her experiences had convinced her she wasn't good at picking husbands. She liked men, though. She liked sex. She was aware of her figure, firm and well proportioned for her age. She had liked Seth and had wanted to sleep with him, maybe wanted something more than that too. When she made a pass at him, she didn't know that he was seeing a girl he met at law school. He later told her that and she wasn't sure if that was the real reason for turning her down or if he was just telling her that to be kind. Probably being kind. He was a kind man.

His brother did not pretend to be a kind man. He was a mercenary and a thief. She owed him nothing.

So why had she lied for him?

Was it because he was Seth's brother? Was it because he was good-looking? Was it because she believed that somewhere beneath that cold exterior there was a human being? Christ, this was how women got involved with guys in prison. A man breaks into your home and you let him take you to dinner and talk you into helping him. Seth himself would shake his head at it.

But maybe the problem wasn't Bridger. Maybe the problem was Gage.

She hadn't intended to lie for Bridger. But somehow when Gage had asked her if she had seen him, it had just seemed smart not to tell him. At that moment she did not trust Gage. . . . Funny, because she had planned to ask Gage what he knew about Michael Hammond. And now she decided she wouldn't.

Brian kissed her on the mouth when he greeted her at the restaurant. Chris pursed her lips so that he wouldn't be able to slip his tongue in. He smiled broadly at her and said, "How you doing, sweetheart?" Christ.

Chris said, "Thanks for meeting me."

Brian was dressed in his brown uniform. He put his Oakley sunglasses on the table.

His hair was more gray now than black and he had a bit of a pot belly going, but he was still handsome. A tall, good-looking man who swaggered and grinned and made a point of smiling at every pretty woman he saw. When Chris was younger, she was flattered that he had picked her. She had always felt she was a little plain. God, had she been that impressionable?

Brian said, "Anything for you."

He raised his fingers to the waitress, summoning her. Which was bad enough. But then when the young lady, who might have been all of nineteen, came to the table, Brian gave her the full piano row of his teeth and said, "How you doing?" Christ, flirting with a kid.

Brian said, "Give me a large iced tea and a tuna melt. What do you want, Chris?"

"Just some toast and coffee," Chris said. She hoped the waitress didn't think they were together.

Brian said, "Is that all? Aren't you hungry?"

"Not very," she said.

With the waitress still there, Brian said, "You look thinner than when we were together. You been working out?"

"Less starch in my diet," Chris said. To the waitress she said, "Thank you."

The waitress went away and Brian said, "You miss me?"

"Sure," Chris said. "How's your wife?"

"She's okay. She wants to go back to school."

"Back to school? What for?"

"Get a nursing degree."

"How old is she now?"

"She's thirty-three. It's not too late."

"No, I guess not. But you guys have a two-year-old."

"You worked when Ellie was that age."

"That's because I had to."

Brian smiled again, like the memory was something they should both be fond of. "We had some good times, didn't we?"

*Not really,* Chris thought. She said, "Sometimes. How's the job going?"

Brian was working as a security guard at a junior college. Somehow he had managed to keep his hands off the coeds. He said, "Going good. They might let me teach a course on criminal justice."

"Are you kidding?" Chris said, a little too quickly.

"Don't be too surprised," Brian said. He seemed genuinely wounded. He always had been a little sensitive.

"I'm sorry," Chris said. "I'm sure that'll

be great. I'm sure you'd be very good at that."

"It isn't finalized yet. We'll see how it goes."

"Brian, the lunch is on me, okay?"

"Okay."

"I called you because I wanted to ask you a favor. Do you remember an officer named Michael Hammond?"

"Michael Hammond . . . black guy?"

"Yeah."

". . . oh, I think so. Oh, yeah. He's an asshole."

"Why do you say that?"

"I remember when he first came on patrol. The first year he was okay, kept in the background, kept his mouth shut. Then his second year he acted like he'd been on patrol for ten years. Knew all the answers. You know the type."

"Type?"

"I don't mean black, if that's where you're going. I mean he had the sergeant's mouth, patrolman's ass syndrome that a lot of young cops get, black and white. He got in trouble a few years ago for sexually harassing a dispatcher. They did an IA and gave him a letter of reprimand. A few months after that, he got investigated for assaulting a guy on a traffic stop. He said the guy he pulled over was white and had called him a nigger. The complainant, a white guy, denied saying that. He said Hammond was verbally abusive and all he'd said to him was 'take it easy' or words to that effect. There was no videotape so they gave Hammond the benefit of the doubt and cleared him. But . . . it became sort of a racial thing at the department. A lot of the white officers thought he had gotten away with something. The black officers thought he should have been cleared. Things were kind of tense for a while. Eventually the patrol lieutenants ordered the officers to stop talking about it."

"What did you think?"

"I thought he was guilty. I mean, that wasn't the first time people had heard of him going a little overboard. But . . . you know. It might have been one of those in-between things."

"What do you mean?"

"Okay, maybe the complainant didn't use the n-word. But maybe he looked at Hammond the wrong way. Like his face was saying, what do you want, *boy?* And for Hammond that was just as bad. But . . . it's hard to know."

"You didn't like him, though?"

"No, I didn't like him. After he was

cleared on that incident he was partnered with a guy named Dean Coates."

"Coates?"

"Yeah. He's black too. After that . . . well, I don't know. Seems like after that incident, Hammond didn't have many white friends at the department. Sometimes, you want to think things have gotten better and they haven't."

Chris regarded Brian. He wasn't all bad. He had actually been a pretty diligent, thoughtful police officer most of the time. If only he could have kept his pants on. But he wasn't the only cop to suffer from that problem. The stress of police work often brewed paranoia and sexual recklessness. Now that she was no longer angry at him, she could remember some of the things she had liked about him. She knew plenty of cops who avoided using the word *nigger* for fear of getting fired but were stone racists all the same. Brian was not one of them, whatever else could be said about him.

Chris said, "Did all the black cops take Hammond's side?"

"No. As I recall, most of the ones who were closer to his age did, while the ones who were older were less likely to. It seems that that's how it was. But you can't read everyone's mind. Like I said, after a while, we were told not to discuss it."

"What's this Coates like?"

"He's a lot easier to deal with. Knows how to deal with people. He's a lot smarter than Hammond. I think I heard that after I was gone they gave Coates his own unit. Special Investigations or something like that. I think Hammond is under Coates's command now."

*After I was gone* . . . Brian would not acknowledge that he had been terminated. Well, let him have that.

Chris said, "What does the unit do?"

"I don't know."

He seemed deflated now. Disappointed that he didn't know. He was no longer in the departmental loop. Working security at a junior college and maybe convincing himself it was something.

Chris reached across the table and touched his hand.

"It's okay," she said. "Thanks for helping me."

She kissed Brian on the cheek before she left the restaurant. She continued her home visits. Late afternoon she returned to her office. She checked her e-mails. One from her daughter that she gave a quick reply to, saying she was at work but would call her later. Katy, the daughter she had had with Brian. A good kid, though she seemed to spend most of her freshman year partying. Chris resisted the impulse to type, *Don't get pregnant. I'm too young to be a grandmother.*

She spent the better part of an hour reviewing the files she had inherited from Seth. Most of them were small-time offenders — low-level meth dealers, thieves and a couple of prostitutes who had been dumb enough to deal crack. Chris had long become accustomed to the grind. She did not delude herself into thinking she was saving any of these people. She just kept shuffling them through the system as best she could.

A few minutes before five her cell phone rang. It was Bridger.

She said, "You got a cell phone?"

"Yeah. I'd rather not have one. But you asked."

"I appreciate it."

Bridger asked, "Did you find anything out about the cop?"

"A little. I'd rather not discuss it on the phone. Can you meet me?"

"At your house?"

"No. Not at my house. There's a bar called St. Michael's Alley near the airport. Can you find it?"

"Sure."

"See you there in about an hour and a half."

# TWENTY-FOUR

Chris said, "I don't want you to buy me dinner."

Bridger said, "Aren't you hungry?"

"No, I'm not hungry."

There were two parts of St. Michael's Alley. The front part was the dining area. Tables and chairs in full view of the kitchen grill. The back part had the bar with a lowered dingy ceiling and red vinyl–topped tables. A greasy, smoky, working-class place. Fox News Network on the television behind the bar with the sound muted. Footage of senators questioning officials of the college BCS for some reason.

Bridger shrugged. It seemed like she was still angry at him.

Chris sipped from a glass of scotch and told him what she had found out.

Bridger said, "How did you find this out?"

"From my ex-husband. He used to be a Seattle police officer."

"Used to be," Bridger said. "Is he retired?"

Chris sighed. "You could say that."

Bridger looked at the bottles stacked behind the bar. He said, "That's not much."

"Well, fuck," Chris said. "It's all he knew. Look, I'm doing what I can."

"I know. But is there something else? What are these guys into now?"

"I don't know. They're black cops working at a department with a majority of white officers. So they're unpopular."

"I thought this was a progressive city."

"It is. But some things . . . well, I don't know."

"The guy with Hammond was black too. I wonder if it was Coates."

"Which one did most of the talking?"

"The one that wasn't Hammond. He told me to leave town or he'd kill me. I guess they sent Hammond to watch me the next day to make sure I'd leave."

"You should have left."

Bridger asked, "Did you look into his offenders?"

"I looked into the ones that were assigned to me. I didn't find anything."

"Okay," Bridger said. He stood up.

Chris said, "You leaving?"

"Yeah. You said that was all you had."

"All right," she said. She hadn't expected

him to leave her. He started to move away. Chris said, "Wait a minute."

"Yeah?"

Chris said, "Is that it? That's all you want from me?"

"Well, yeah," Bridger said. "You said you'd done all you could. I believe you."

"You've got two names. That's it."

"It's a start," Bridger said.

"You don't want any more help from me?"

"No," Bridger said. "Thanks, though."

She looked at him for a while. Then she said, "Well, good luck with everything."

"Thanks again."

"And be careful, okay?"

"I will."

Bridger moved through the parked cars seeking out the rented Ford. A man stepped out from behind a van, looked at him and said, "How's it going?"

Bridger stopped. "Fine. We met, didn't we?"

Marlon Gage took a pistol out of his jacket and held it on Bridger. "Yeah," he said. "We've met. Over here."

He motioned Bridger to a Pontiac Firebird and told him to put his hands on the roof.

Bridger said, "What are you doing?"

"Put your hands on the roof."

Bridger did so. Gage frisked him. He found the .357 revolver in his pocket and took it out.

"What are you doing with this, asshole?"

Bridger didn't answer.

Gage said, "Carrying a concealed weapon without a permit." Gage put the revolver in his jacket pocket. "All right," he said. "Get in the car. No, the driver's side."

That's when Bridger knew he was in trouble. He hesitated for a moment, waiting to be told he was under arrest, waiting to be read his rights, waiting, mostly, for Chris Rider to come outside and see what this was about and maybe put a stop to it. How much drink did she have left?

"Supposing I say no?" Bridger said.

"Then I'll shoot you here. Put that gun back on you after."

"And you'd rather do that later," Bridger said.

"Just get in the car."

Bridger got in the car and started it. He pulled it out of the parking lot and on the road.

Bridger said, "Is this an arrest?"

"No, no. We just want to talk."

"Who's we? Coates? Hammond?"

Gage said, "Make a right here. Get on the Interstate. Keep it within the speed limits."

They were quiet for a while, driving amongst night traffic.

Bridger said, "Did you kill Seth?"

"Shut up."

"Did you? Just tell me."

"No, I didn't kill him."

"Who did? Was it Hammond? Coates?"

"I don't know."

"Yeah you do. You wouldn't be doing this otherwise."

"Shut up."

Bridger said, "You say you didn't kill him, I believe you. I don't think you've ever killed anyone."

"Just drive," Gage said, hitting him on the head with the gun. "And keep your mouth shut."

They drove for a few miles then Gage directed him to get off the interstate. Soon they were at an empty park next to a lake. Gage ordered him out of the car and they walked to a picnic area. Gage told him to sit on the top of the picnic table with his feet on the bench. Then he told Bridger to put his hands on his knees.

Gage stepped back about ten feet and held the gun on him with one hand. With the other hand he took a cell phone out of his pocket and dialed a number.

Gage said, "Yeah . . . I got him. I'm

here . . . Where are you?"

Gage was talking tough. He was proud of himself, having taken the mark on his own, telling his people they needed to be here too.

*But why?* Bridger thought. *Why couldn't he just do it himself?*

Gage said, "Okay, then." He folded his phone and put it back in his pocket.

Bridger said, "Kind of a public place, isn't it?"

Gage said, "You see anyone else here?"

"Who's coming?"

"You'll see."

"When they get here, what are you going to do? Stand there and watch them do it?"

Gage shook his head, not wanting to talk about it anymore. He said, "It's your fault."

"What?"

"It's your fault, man," Gage said. "You brought this on yourself."

"Because I didn't leave?"

"You were warned. They gave you a chance?"

"What about Seth? Was he warned? Was he given a chance?"

Headlights approaching now, a car coming down the gravel road. An unmarked four-door sedan. The brights flicking on now, illuminating the Pontiac, then the car moving past and the lights shining on Bridger and Gage. The car now peeling off the road and driving on the grass.

Bridger glanced at Gage and thought about launching off the table but Gage was aware of him, pointing the gun at him, saying, "Stay there, man."

Then the car door opened. Chris Rider got out.

# TWENTY-FIVE

Marlon Gage's voice was raised. "Chris, what are you doing here?" He still held the gun on Bridger.

"What are *you* doing here? Marlon, what's going on?"

"Nothing," Gage said. "Chris, get out of here. Get in the car and get out of here."

"Why? Marlon, put that gun down."

"Chris, goddammit, get out of here."

Bridger said, "Chris, he's going to kill me. His pals are on their way."

"Shut up!" Gage said. "Chris, get the fuck out of here."

Chris Rider drew her service weapon. She pointed it at Bridger who raised his hands. Then she pointed it at Gage.

Gage said, "Don't. Chris, what are —"

"Holster that weapon, Marlon. Holster yours and I'll holster mine."

"I can't do that. Chris, get out of here."

Bridger said, "Tell her who's coming, Marlon."

"Shut up."

Bridger said, "He's telling you to leave because if you're here, they'll have to kill you too."

"I said shut the fuck *up*."

Chris said, "Oh God, Marlon. What have you gotten into?"

Bridger said, "He's right, Chris. We need to go." He slid off the picnic table. Gage stepped back, still holding the gun on him. *Shoot him,* Gage thought. But Chris was here now. How would he explain it to her?

"Get back up there," Gage said.

"Let's go, Chris," Bridger said. "This man's got a meeting." Bridger started to walk to the passenger side of Chris's car.

"Stop," Gage said. It was happening too quickly. *"Stop."*

Gage raised the gun to fire and Chris shot him in the shoulder. Gage screamed and fell down. He raised the gun and fired at Chris and she fired back at him twice, both shots in the chest. Then fired again.

Stillness.

Chris walked over to Gage and knelt beside him. She took his gun away from him. Gage's eyes fluttered for a moment. Then they stopped. He was dead.

Bridger said, "Chris."

"You shut up," Chris said. "You shut your goddamn mouth."

"Chris, we have to leave. Men are coming here to kill me. I don't know how many. They'll kill you too."

"We're not going anywhere. Put your hands on the hood of the car. I'm arresting you."

"Chris. Let's go."

Chris turned at the sound of another car approaching. Coming quickly now.

"Chris, please."

She looked at the car coming at them, heard the sound of the engine being raced, saw the car powering toward them. She moved to the driver's door. Bridger got in the car next to her. She started the car and put it in gear and hit the gas. She circled around the bench, spinning tires on grass. Now the other car was close enough to discern the make. A Dodge Charger, the brights on as it veered off the road and onto the grass, coming straight for them. The cars hurtled toward each other, Bridger grabbing the arm rest and Chris tightened her grip on the steering wheel, the distance between them closing and then Chris went to the right of the Charger and the Charger moved with them as they passed, the

Charger making contact with Chris's Chevy, knocking it askew. The Chevy fishtailed but Chris kept it under control and the Charger skidded into a one eighty, swung around, and raced back after them.

Chris made a right turn coming out of the park. She drove fast down a two-lane road lined by trees. In the rearview mirror she saw the Charger come out of the park after them. She pressed the accelerator down, but she knew the Charger probably had a bigger engine. The road began to curve and she felt the tires lose their grip as she went through the first turn.

"Easy," Bridger said. "You go off the road, they'll catch us."

"I know how to drive."

But on the next turn the Chevy skidded into the oncoming lane and she had to wrestle with the wheel to keep from sliding off the road. The Charger's high beams reflected off the rearview mirror. And then there was a crack and a hole appeared in the back window. The road went into a long arc and Chris tried to ease the car into it but about three quarters of the way through the Chevy went into another skid and slid into the oncoming lane as a pickup came from the other direction. The pickup's horn blared and it went halfway off the road, struggling not to flip over and the Chevy slid through the passage and Chris regained control of it. The pickup slipped back onto the road and went into the oncoming lane, an overcorrection, which put it in front of the Dodge Charger. The driver of the Charger stood on the brakes and cranked the wheel to his right, putting the car in the ditch.

Chris slowed at the next intersection for a red light, saw no traffic, and punched it through. She drove to the next intersection on a busy thoroughfare. She waited for the light, drove through the intersection and kept straight. They passed through a commercial strip of chain restaurants and soon were in a quiet residential neighborhood. She parked the car in front of a dark house and cut the lights. After about a minute she turned off the ignition.

Bridger said, "I saw them go in the ditch. I think we're okay."

She didn't answer.

"Chris?"

She pulled her gun back out and pointed it at him.

Bridger looked at the gun. The barrel was level with his stomach. Then he looked at her. He said, "You still going to arrest me?"

Her voice shaking, she said, "You made

that happen. You made me shoot my friend."

"Your friend was going to shoot me. Or hold me until those guys got there so they could do it."

"You don't know that."

"Who was that chasing us then?"

"I don't know."

"Don't you want to know?" Bridger said. "They'd've killed you too. And Gage would have stood there and watched it happen."

"Fuck you. You don't know that. He wouldn't have let anything happen to me."

"You sure?" Bridger said, "Let's say you're right. Let's say he would have protected you. Would it have been okay if they had just killed me? Would that have made it all right?"

"I've never . . . for God's sake . . . Marlon . . ."

"You've never killed anyone."

Chris lowered the gun and put it on her lap. She looked down and shook her head.

"I'm not like you," she said. "It doesn't come easy for me."

"No," Bridger said. "You're not like me." Gently, he reached over and took the gun from her lap and set it on the console. "I'm sorry," he said.

Tears welled in her eyes. "You don't understand," she said. "I shot my friend. I shot an officer of the law. I'm going to lose everything. My daughters . . ."

"You're not going to lose everything. We'll work something out."

"We'll work something out," she said, like it was the dumbest statement in the world. "How? How will 'we' do that?"

"I'll think of something. Listen to me, if you hadn't come along, I would be dead now. Gage or his friends, it would have happened. Would you have preferred that outcome?"

She waited a moment before answering. Then looked at him and sort of smiled. "I'm not sure," she said.

Bridger laughed. He said, "Well, at least you're honest."

"Jesus," she said. "That's the first time I've heard you laugh. I can't say I like it."

"Sorry. Okay. You've got two options. One, you don't do anything. Gage will be discovered and the police will be called in. No one knows you were there except us and the guys who came after you. They may have an interest in keeping quiet about it."

"Or they may report it. Make an anonymous call. My gun is examined and I'm toast."

"Right. Which leads to the second option. You call it in. And tell them the truth. That you killed Gage because he was about to kill me. Tell them everything."

"What do I tell them about you?"

Bridger said, "You tell them I ran away."

Chris Rider took the gun off the console and shook her head. "No," she said. "I'll need you to back me up. You owe me one."

# Twenty-Six

He spent the night in jail.

After Chris took him back to the park and put him in handcuffs and called the cops, he told them all he wanted to and when they got shitty with him he told him if they wanted to try to make him change his story they'd have to talk to his lawyer. A cop or two shouted in his face and another told him if he wanted to be stupid about it that was his choice. He was put in a municipal cell around midnight. The arresting officer enjoyed telling him he would be going to county in the morning with all the other shitbirds.

Around seven A.M. two uniformed jailers came with a plainclothes detective. The jailers got into the cell and put him in a belly chain and handcuffs attached to same. They led him out of the cell and out of the lockdown area. When they got to the end of the cage one of the jailers asked the plainclothes cop if he wanted help escorting the prisoner. The plainclothes cop said no and thanked the jailer by name.

As they walked down the hall and into the elevator, Bridger regarded the plainclothes cop. Big white guy with black hair and a mustache. A traditional-looking, rumpled, ugly cop, the sort who had no expression on his face when he cracked a joke and probably smiled when he was about to hit you.

In the elevator, Mitch Carnahan said, "So how do you like our city?"

Bridger looked at him and didn't answer.

Carnahan said, "Been to the Space Needle? It's quite a sight if you can get past the crowds."

Bridger thought, a country boy. Came in from the eastern part of the state to take a job with a big-city Po-lice Department. Probably wasn't much different from a guy from western Pennsylvania. Or West Virginia.

Bridger said, "I called my lawyer last night in Baltimore. He said he was going to find someone here to come see me. I was wondering if you knew anything about that."

Carnahan said, "Lawyer?"

"Yeah."

"You think one would come that soon?"

"My lawyer guaranteed he'd get me one within two hours."

"Hmmm. Well, maybe he did. But if he did, the man's probably waiting for you at county now. That's where you're supposed to be."

Bridger looked at this cop again. He was easygoing, not putting on any muscle. He didn't seem to be in any hurry.

Bridger said, "I didn't see you there last night."

"You mean when you were arrested?"

"Yeah. I don't remember seeing you there."

"I must have been sleeping in the car," Carnahan said.

*Shit,* Bridger thought. A *smart* country boy. They were the worst kind. He'd known guys like this in the Navy.

They got off the elevator on the basement floor. There was no one in the halls, no sign of work activity. They walked down a corridor and Carnahan rapped three times on a gray door.

From inside, a man said, "Yeah."

"It's me," Carnahan said.

The door unlocked and they walked into a storage room. There was a middle-aged black man in plainclothes. He looked Bridger over the way a man would a horse, clinically, taking his time about it, and Bridger thought, *homicide.*

"Okay," the black guy said. "Bring him back here."

They walked through stacked boxes of closed files, rounded a corner where there were two metal folding chairs waiting for them.

The black guy said, "Take the cuffs off him."

"You sure?" Carnahan said.

"Sure I'm sure," the black guy said. "Mr. Bridger here is a professional cat burglar. He's not going to try to rush us."

Carnahan removed the belly chain and cuffs and told Bridger to sit in one of the chairs. The black guy sat in the other.

"My name is Harris."

A few moments passed, then Bridger said, "How do I know that?"

Charney Harris said, "What do you mean?"

"How do I know you're who you say you are? Maybe your name is Coates."

Harris grinned. "Smart man. Shall I show you some identification?"

"Yeah."

He showed Bridger his badge and his police commission card. "Okay?" he said.

"Okay," Bridger said.

Harris said, "I want to talk to you about Coates, though. What do you know about him?"

Bridger looked at the black detective. His eyes roamed about the stacked boxes and the gray cement walls. He said, "This doesn't look like an interrogation room. There's no two-way mirror. Have you got a recording device somewhere?"

Harris said, "What do you think?"

"I'm not sure," Bridger said.

"Right," Harris said. Harris seemed to study him for a moment. Then he said, "Your little brother was murdered. You think Coates did it?"

For a while Bridger didn't say anything. He looked at the black detective and wondered if he'd heard him right. One cop talking about another cop killing someone. Killing his brother. Asking or telling.

Bridger said, "I'm trying to find out."

"What proof do you have?"

"Why do you want to know?"

"You were arrested for unlawfully leaving the scene of a crime."

"I can explain that. I have explained it."

"Not to their satisfaction. The department can find something else on you if they work hard enough at it. And you've got a record."

"I did my time, all of it. Put me back in

my cell and I'll be out of here in twelve hours."

"You that confident?"

"My lawyer knows what he's doing."

"Maybe," Harris said. "But maybe you can walk out of here this morning."

"And leave the state," Bridger said. "Right?"

Harris shook his head. "Wrong."

Harris picked up a folder and took a photo out of it. He handed the photo to Bridger. Harris said, "You recognize him?"

Bridger looked at the photo. "No."

"That's Dean Coates. Take a good look at it."

"Here's another one," Harris said. "Recognize him?"

It was a photo of a black police officer in uniform. It was Hammond.

Harris said, "Him, I think you know. He was involved in a vehicle collision recently, abducted and assaulted and battered. Using a vehicle as a weapon qualifies as assault with a deadly weapon. And then there's kidnapping a police officer and that's a federal offense. You'd be looking at ten years. And that's federal time, which means you'd do all of it. Here are some more."

Harris handed Bridger three more photos. Names attached to faces. Jim Patterson,

Charles Eatherly, Alex Dupree. He went back to the one of Jim Patterson. Studied it and matched it with what he remembered of the man who had beat him up in the alley and threatened to kill him.

Bridger handed the photos back.

"Right," Bridger said. "What does Hammond say?"

The black cop and the white cop exchanged a look. Harris said, "What if I told you he identified you?"

"I'd say you were full of shit."

"And why's that?"

"Because if he had, I wouldn't be here with you."

Carnahan started paring his fingernails with the point of a file extending from his penknife. Without looking at Bridger or Harris, he said, "Tell him about the theft."

Harris said, "Oh, yeah. Okay, three, four weeks ago, there was a shipment of ecstasy stolen near the Canadian border. We don't know how many tabs were taken. The dealers didn't report the theft, of course. But a couple of people in State Narcotics got wind of this. Nobody knows where it is now. Maybe it was stolen by a rival group of dealers, maybe by one of the Mexican cartels. Who knows? There's so many dealers out there. The free market at work, you know.

Ever steal narcotics? . . . No, didn't think so. You steal it, you have to sell it, right? And that means you'd have to deal with people in the narcotics trade. A smart guy like you wouldn't do that, would you?"

"Haven't yet," Bridger said.

"No," Harris said. "You like to keep it simple, don't you? Concentrate on diamonds and gold, that sort of thing, work with as few people as possible. You'd make much more money in narcotics. Much more. But then, you don't live as long. A lot higher risk."

Bridger said, "That's what I hear."

"I heard some things too," Harris said. "I heard about a guy who got set up by the mob in Philadelphia. They framed him for the murder of a judge and then they tried to kill him. Four or five of those mobsters got killed themselves. The feds never got the guy, but there were a couple of Philly cops figured this guy's hands were pretty dirty. But they figured it was okay if the guy got away with it. It helped clean things up. They figured maybe this guy did them a favor. One of the cops pointed out that after this guy finished doing what he needed to do, he left town and didn't come back. They liked that."

Bridger took it in. He said, "You want me

to stay?"

Harris said, "You're going to stay, either way. You help us, you stay here for a while. Until we get this thing figured out. You don't help us, you stay here a long time."

Bridger looked from the black cop to the white cop. Then back to the black cop. He said, "You want me to kill Coates."

Harris turned to Carnahan. "Did I say that?"

Carnahan shook his head.

Harris said, "No, I didn't think I had. Maybe Coates and his crew didn't steal that ecstasy shipment. And maybe Coates didn't have anything to do with your brother's murder. Maybe his crew wasn't in the car that chased you last night."

"Maybe," Bridger said. "And maybe you're the one that killed Seth. And now you want to use me to get rid of a cop you don't want around, take the heat off you."

"That's good thinking," Harris said. "I'll tell you what. You find any proof that I had anything to do with your brother, you can find me yourself. I think you're the sort who knows how to find people."

Bridger said, "You say it was Coates who killed Seth. Why not arrest him?"

Harris said, "Truth is, we weren't sure he killed your brother. We didn't see a connection until you got here. The man who you say abducted you, what do you know about him?"

"Marlon Gage," Carnahan said.

"Yeah, Gage," Harris said. "What do you know about him?"

Bridger said, "He worked with my brother."

"Your brother say much about him?"

"My brother and I didn't talk much."

"What about Officer Rider?"

"What about her?"

"Did she have something going on with Gage?"

"I doubt it."

"But you don't know, do you?"

"No, I suppose I don't."

Harris said, "Marlon Gage and Dean Coates grew up in the same neighborhood. They went to the same high school. You think Gage was going to kill you?"

"I think he was going to hold me at the park until his friends got there."

"And then what?"

"Then they would kill me."

Harris said, "But Officer Rider got there before they did."

"That's right."

"And killed Officer Gage."

"Yeah."

"That's your story and you're sticking to it."

"That's what happened," Bridger said.

Harris said, "She told the police she shot him because he was going to kill you."

"That's right."

"Not to protect herself."

"No."

"She should have said it was in her own defense," Harris said. "Not yours. It would have been better that way. Better for her. The police, they're wondering why she'd bother protecting a criminal from an officer of the law. They're wondering if her interest in you is something . . . personal."

"It's not."

"I'm wondering," Harris said, "if her interest is something else."

Bridger didn't respond to that.

Harris said, "After all, white people can be corrupted too. Believe it or not."

"Hmmm," Bridger said. "One problem with that."

"What?"

"If she were mixed up with Coates, she'd have let them kill me. Or done it herself. But something else. It would mean Seth was probably involved too. And that's not possible."

"You don't know that," Harris said. "You

said yourself you hadn't talked to him in some time. Maybe a long time. A wise man once asked who among us knows his brother? You don't really know, do you? You stayed here to find out who killed your brother. But what if you find out something you don't like? What if you find out that Seth was involved in something dirty? Then you'll have to go home with your tail between your legs. Sometimes a false memory is better than the truth."

"Yeah, it's a gamble," Bridger said. "But what's it to you? You told me I have to stay and help you."

"Yeah, that's about the size of it. Well, like I said, we don't have much of a case against Coates. Maybe you can find things out we can't. Maybe you've got more of an incentive than we do. Maybe you can even find the missing tabs of ecstasy. Shake things up."

"And report back to you?"

"No," Harris said. "But we'll be around." Harris turned to Carnahan and said, "Anything else you can think of?"

Carnahan shook his head.

Harris said, "You're free to go."

"Be safe," Carnahan said, unsmiling.

# TWENTY-SEVEN

Eatherly was the first one to start losing his nerve.

He insisted that their license tag had been taken down by the thief or by the lady. Patterson was folding his arms again, but letting Dean do the talking because Dean was always better at the voice of reason stuff. Dean said, "Man, they took off as soon as they saw us coming. What do you think, she took the time to write down a license tag? In the dark, in a panic?"

Eatherly said, "She's a cop. She's supposed to notice things like that."

Coates said, "She's a goddamn parole officer and she's out of her league."

They were in a parking lot with a taco truck selling the best tamales on the north side. The vendors barely spoke English, but the men stood far enough away. Coates holding a cup of Dr Pepper with a straw in it, trying to calm down Eatherly, but using the occasion to let the other members of his crew know everything was okay. Dupree, Patterson and Hammond were there too.

Eatherly said, "The police report says she killed Gage. Not him, her."

"How do you know that?"

"I saw the report," Eatherly said. "Have you?"

"Yeah, I saw it," Coates said, though he hadn't. Coates said, "Just because she told the reporting officer that don't mean it's true. Bridger killed Gage. Don't you see that?"

"But the report —"

"Fuck the report. It doesn't say anything about us."

"It gives her statement. She says she was pursued by a black sedan."

"That's it, right? A black sedan?"

". . . yeah."

"Well, that ain't shit, brother. No descriptions of you, me, Michael. Alex and Jim weren't there."

"They should have been," Eatherly said.

Patterson said, "What?" His voice sharp.

Coates said, "Never mind that. Boys. We're all in this together. We all got alibis. Charles, you weren't there and neither were me or Michael. Now what have you got to worry about?"

Eatherly said, "It's bad luck, man. Gage was our connection to Ramos. Now that he's gone, they'll assign someone else to watch over Ramos. And then where will we be?"

"They're not going to reassign Eddie for a while. And by the time they do, we won't need him anymore."

There was a silence among them. Another car pulling into the lot, three fat white guys getting out and walking to the line in front of the taco truck.

Eatherly said, "Okay. Say you're right. Say Ramos is around to help us seal the deal. But the next time Ramos violates his parole — and he will — what do you think he's going to do? You think he's going to keep his mouth shut and go back to jail? After what he knows about you?"

Coates was aware of all his men waiting for an answer. He looked them over, all of them, making eye contact with one or two, but not having the nerve to do them all.

Coates said, "I've thought about that already. When it's done, I'll take care of Ramos. We won't need him anymore."

Eatherly said, "You'll take care of him? Well, that's fine, brother. But if Ramos is tight with the Los Cholos, they're liable to come after us if we kill him."

*Shit.* Now Coates saw the uncertainty on the faces of Dupree and Hammond. Coates said, "Look motherfucker, you want to take over? Is that what you're saying?"

"No, Dean, I just —"

"You want to back out?"

". . . no."

"Then shut the fuck up," Coates said. "Ramos is just a go-between. A middle man, he don't mean shit to the Cholos. Now, everybody just be cool. We're all going to go back to work like nothing happened. Because nothing has. Okay?"

They walked back to their cars, Eatherly shaking his head as he did so. Coates decided to ignore it. If not for the presence of the others, Coates might have capped him for the disrespect. Patterson lingered and when he was alone with Coates, he spoke to him in a smooth, diplomatic tone.

Patterson acknowledged the backs of the men walking away. "They're still with you," he said.

Coates said, "And you?"

Patterson said, "You doubt me, Dean?"

Coates studied Patterson's stolid expression for a moment. Coates said, "No, man. I'm sorry."

Patterson said, "Like you said, we're all in this together."

"Yeah."

"But I was thinking," Patterson said, "what about the thief? He's in county now and what if he starts talking?"

"He doesn't know anything," Coates said.

Patterson said, "He's seen my face."

"So what? You think they're going to show him your mug shot?"

"He found Michael."

"Michael got stupid, let his guard down. You're better than that. I'd like to see what happened to him if he found you."

"Now you're blowing smoke up my behind," Patterson said.

Coates said, "I'm just saying you can handle him, that's all."

"Right." Patterson was smiling, going along with Coates in his way, but still letting him know he wasn't fooling him at all. "Well, my friend, I'd feel a whole lot better if they let him out."

"So would I," Coates said. "I wonder if they'll let him post bond."

There was no bond. There was no record of bond being posted or even set. No arraignment, no initial appearance before a judge. Daniel Bridger was released from the city jail as if he had been found passed out drunk on a street corner and slept it off in a cell.

What happened?

Coates found out about it after making a few surreptitious calls. He wanted to be relieved. The man was out and now all they had to do was find him and put his ass down. But it was too easy. Something wasn't right. The man had been present when an officer of the law had been shot and killed. They didn't just let people spend one night in jail for that. Not a man who had done time. Not a man who police believed had killed people in another state. They didn't just let a man like that *out.*

The report said that Chris Rider had killed Gage. But that couldn't be true. The woman was a fucking parole officer. They never shot people. They filled out reports and turned them over to the district attorney's office and had probations revoked. They weren't cops, they were state employees. Civil servants. Bridger had to have shot Gage and somehow got the woman to cover for him.

*Fucking Marlon,* Coates thought. He should have called him immediately. He wanted to do it alone. Coates remembered Marlon's voice on the telephone when he called to tell him he had apprehended

241

Bridger. Very proud of himself, using a cop's tone. Like he wanted to prove to them he was as good as they were. Marlon. Like a lot of men at probation and parole, he had wanted to be a cop but couldn't get hired. He hadn't been able to pass the physical. And the truth was, the man wasn't that bright, though he had always thought he was. Coates remembered riding in a car with Marlon and someone had rushed past them and cut in quick and Marlon had sped up behind him like he was going to arrest the man or something. Coates had said, "What are you doing?" And then had to talk Marlon out of chasing the guy down. Marlon trying to prove something then too. . . . No, he wouldn't miss Marlon much.

Though it was Marlon who brought Eddie Ramos to his attention. That had been luck. Eddie Ramos, the mid-level dealer and general shitbird Mexican who had connections to the Los Cholos cartel. Marlon had read Eddie's file and told Coates he might be worth looking at. Marlon had not known what a find he had in Ramos. He had gotten lucky, but he had wanted a full share of the take when it was done. Well, that was one share less they would have to pay.

Three million dollars. That's what they had coming to them. Three million dollars to be split among him and Patterson and Dupree and Hammond and Eatherly. Three million . . . to be split, what, evenly? That wouldn't be right. He had set this whole thing up. Should he have to split it evenly with the rest of them? What had they done, really?

But then he remembered that none of his crew knew what the number was. He had talked alone with Ramos. If Ramos were dead after the deal was done, none of them would know how much he got. Coates remembered paying a guy fourteen hundred cash to take a tree stump out of his backyard. The guy had a crew of three men, men who looked like they'd come out of the homeless day care center and probably did. When they were finished, the leader asked Coates to pay him out of sight of his crew. Coates smiled then.

It could work the same way here. Take the money from Ernesto Aguilar, the Los Cholos underboss, give the boys a hundred grand a piece in cash. Lot of tax-free money. They shouldn't have reason to complain. Which would leave Coates with two and a half million and change.

Money he was meant to have. Dean Coates believed that as much as he had ever believed anything. When he was in junior high and high school, he was revered as young gifted athletes usually are. He was accommodated and praised and often worshipped. He was the good black athlete white people took pride in admiring. He was handsome and graceful and he had the best hands in the state. He had caught the pass on the seventy-yard line and run it into the end zone for his second six in the game, winning the state championship. God, what a day that had been. He still remembered how proud his family was when his picture was in *Parade Magazine.* He was destined to be a football star. Everyone said so, and he believed everyone who said so was right.

But the gods give early promise to those they wish to punish, and when Dean Coates's football career puttered out before the age of twenty, he never fully came to terms with it. Two and a half million dollars . . . that should have been his signing bonus after he was drafted by the San Francisco Forty Niners. Instead, he was just another lump-assed cop in Seattle, struggling to support his family and a string of skinny, greedy bitches. He had earned that money and he wasn't going to have some small-time thief from Baltimore keep him from getting it. Not him or his punk-ass little brother.

# Twenty-Eight

He knocked three times, waited and knocked three more before she came to the door. She was wearing medical scrub pants and a white T-shirt with a plaid bathrobe over it. She stared at Bridger for a while.

Then Bridger said, "I thought you'd be here instead of the office."

"You thought right," Chris Rider said.

"They gave you the day off?"

"Yeah," she said. "It's standard procedure when you've been involved in a shooting death. But then they sent an officer over here about an hour ago giving me written notice. I'm on suspension pending an administrative investigation. Paid suspension, but it's still a suspension."

"I'm sorry."

"No, you're not. If you could go back and change things, you wouldn't. You made me shoot Marlon."

"I told you before, I didn't want that to

245

happen."

"I didn't believe you. I still don't. I killed a friend of mine and now I may lose my job. If I'm lucky, I may not have criminal charges filed against me. I still haven't hired a lawyer, but friends — the few friends I have left — are telling me I'm going to have to hire one. You tell me why I should be anything other than sorry I ever met you."

"There's not much I can say," Bridger said. "But I'll tell you this: Marlon Gage was not your friend. If you hadn't have done what you did, he would've let both of us be killed."

"Again, you don't know that."

"I'm as sure of it as I am of anything. You didn't know him as well as you thought."

She glared at him as if that was the harshest thing he had ever said to her. She said, "Just get out of here."

"All right, if you want. But will you let me tell you what I've learned?"

"Why should I?"

"Because it might keep you alive."

He sat at her kitchen table, sipping coffee while he told it to her; the visit from the cops, the theft of the ecstasy, the reputation of Dean Coates. Chris stood against the counter, still in her bathrobe and slippers, forgetting herself for the time being.

Chris said, "Brian said something about him. About Coates. He said Hammond works for him now."

"What do you know about Coates?"

"Never heard of him until this."

"You sure?"

"I just told you." She looked at him for a moment. "You think I'm lying?"

"No. The cops I talked to wondered if you might be involved."

"With corrupt cops?"

"Yeah."

"What did you tell them?"

"I told them I doubted it."

"Well, thanks for the support. Are these guys after me too?"

"No, I think they were just trying to feel me out. I think they want me to think Coates killed Seth for some reason."

"Why?"

"Because they want me to kill Coates."

Silence. The woman with her arms folded staring at Bridger again.

She said, "Did they say that?"

"No. They made a point of not saying it."

"Are you going to do it?"

"I don't know. Coates may not have done anything to Seth. This guy Harris, he's obviously got some personal beef with Coates.

But I'm not going to be used to settle his score."

"What a relief. What *are* you going to do?"

"I'm going to find out what happened. Isn't that what you want?"

Chris Rider shook her head. "I don't know anymore."

Bridger regarded the woman in her bathrobe, her hair still wet from a shower, her neck tan and supple. A good-looking woman apparently unafraid of him, unafraid of telling him what she thought. An uncommon lady.

Bridger said, "I haven't thanked you for what you did."

The woman shook her head again. "It isn't necessary. It was a clean shoot."

"You saved my life." She was still quiet and Bridger said, "How did you know? How did you know he had taken me?"

"I walked out of the club and I saw him put you in his car. If he had put you in the passenger side, I probably wouldn't have done anything. But he put you behind the wheel and it made me stop. Why would he do that? It made me nervous. So I followed you. When you guys got off the interstate, I lost you. That curvy road? I went down that for a while before I turned around and went back to the park and found you."

Bridger said, "If you'd have kept going, all your troubles would be over."

"Yeah, I guess they would." She looked at him and smiled. "Don't ask me if I regret turning around."

"Do you regret turning around?"

"I told you not to ask," she said. They made eye contact. Chris said, "No, I don't regret it. Marlon *was* dirty, wasn't he?"

"He was there," Bridger said. "There wouldn't be any other explanation."

Chris said, "I can't believe he would do that to Seth. That he would have any part of something like that."

"It seems like he did. Although I don't think he killed Seth. I think that was someone else."

Chris said, "A couple of cops are telling you it was Coates, maybe because he did it or maybe because they just don't like him very much and would like to see a thief get rid of him. Or maybe they're just using you to smoke Coates and his people out, catch them in something they can use."

Bridger said, "I was thinking that too."

"Using a thief to catch a thief. And a murderer. You get killed, what's it to them? Worst comes to worst, they can charge Coates with your murder."

"Or wait for another day," Bridger said.

"And Seth." She didn't have to add that the cops didn't much give a shit about him one way or another.

"Yeah," Bridger said. "Seth."

Chris said, "You told the cops I wasn't involved. Did you say that to keep them off balance or because you actually believe it?"

"Because I believe it."

"You believe it . . . something you can see with your heart? A good feeling?"

"No. Because you saved my life. If you were in on it, you wouldn't have done that."

"Maybe I had my own motive for doing it. Maybe I'm clever."

"You're not that clever," Bridger said.

Their eyes did not meet again. Bridger was looking at the table when he said it. It made Chris smile.

Bridger said, "I don't think you should stay here."

"Why not?"

"Because those guys might come looking for you. You're on suspension now. Can you leave town for a few days?"

"I'm not leaving town," she said. "This is my house and I can take care of myself. Besides, if they come here, it'll probably be because they're looking for you."

"Good point," Bridger said. He stood up.

"You're going?"

"Yeah. Listen, I'm grateful for what you're doing for Seth. You're a good friend."

Chris said, "To Seth?"

"Yeah." He didn't know what else it could mean. "I'm going to disappear for a while. Can I call you later?"

"Yes."

Bridger returned to his motel. It was a low-rent place, two stories with steps on the outside and an empty swimming pool in the center of the parking lot. Highway traffic motored by less than a hundred yards away.

He took the .45 from the trunk of the Ford into his room. He made sure it was loaded and chambered before he put it on the nightstand. He locked the front door and put the chain on the door. Then he shoved the desk chair up under the knob. If someone tried to kick the door in they would have to kick more than twice. It would give him some time, maybe.

He lay on the bed and went to sleep.

He awoke about three hours later, surprised he had slept so long. He hadn't slept much the night before. It had been a long time since he'd had to spend the night in jail. He had done a stretch in state prison when he was younger and didn't know much. He hadn't experienced one thing he liked there, though he had met the Chinaman there and the Chinaman had taught him things about stealing he hadn't known before. The Chinaman had told him a man could make good money moving high-end merchandise if he was smart and learned a few simple rules and stuck with them.

One of the rules involved never doing business with the Mob because the Mob would sell you out or kill you in a heartbeat. Another rule was to try to work alone as much as possible. Another rule was to never do business with guys who drank too much or took drugs because they could never be counted on. And another rule was to avoid getting in feuds with criminals as well as cops. The key was to keep a low profile. The Chinaman said cops always knew a hothead when they saw one and they would look for a reason to bust him. He said that when you encountered a cop, always but always be polite and keep your answers short. White or black, a cop would arrest any man who gave them too much mouth and call it disorderly conduct, maybe find more things to charge you with later. Don't mess with cops.

Well, he'd broken that rule. He was now in a full-blown war with crooked police and working with other cops who were probably going to screw him too. Somewhere the Chinaman was shaking his head.

But what was he to do? How does a smart man walk away from his brother? From his own blood? There was no choice but to stay.

Seth had chosen a better path. He had avoided crime and avoided the wrong people. Seth's friends were people like Chris and Elaine. Good people. Seth had done nothing to deserve his fate. If Coates had killed Seth, why had he done it? Harris had told him that Coates and his crew had stolen a load of ecstasy and were looking for a place to unload it. What did that have to do with Seth? What would it have to do with a civil servant parole officer?

What did it have to do with Marlon Gage? Another parole officer. He was not sorry Gage was dead. He was a coward and a shitbird and he had been willing to kill Bridger and almost certainly had something to do with Seth's murder. He was sorry that the woman had had to do it, but it was better that Gage die than him. He might have killed Gage himself if the woman hadn't done it. After he'd asked him some questions. Too late for that now.

Bridger had killed men before. He had done it in self-defense if not self-preservation, and believed he had never done it for reasons of vengeance. He had never killed in what criminologists called the heat of passion. All the people he had killed had been trying to kill him. He had never killed a civilian. Or a cop.

# TWENTY-NINE

Ray Humphreys called Chris around lunchtime. Ray was her union representative. She had never worked in the same district with him, but she knew and respected him. He asked her if it was true she had been served with a notice of an internal administrative investigation and she told him it was.

Ray said, "Have they scheduled you for a formal interview yet?"

Chris said, "No."

Ray said, "I know a good lawyer, a labor guy. I can line you up with him. The union can pay his retainer."

"I appreciate that, Ray."

"If there's a criminal investigation, he might refer you out if it's real serious."

Chris shut her eyes, opened them and said, "Is there going to be a criminal investigation?"

"I've asked," Ray said, "but they're not telling me. The DS is saying things like,

'Well, I don't know. This is troubling.' But that doesn't mean anything. Sometimes they say that stuff to try to scare you into resigning so they don't have to bother with the admin investigation."

"I'm not resigning," Chris said.

"No one's advising that, least of all me. You do that, they win."

"My pension —"

"Chris, listen to me. You are not resigning. They don't have a strong case against you. Don't psych yourself out with things that may never happen."

"Okay, Ray."

"Listen, we don't have to talk about it now, but I always thought Marlon was a bad guy anyway."

"You did?"

"Yeah. I worked with him in District Six years ago. He was investigated for sexually assaulting one of his offenders. The allegation was, he threatened to file an app to revoke on one of his female offenders if she didn't give him head." Ray paused. "Sorry."

Chris wasn't offended by the head comment. She was a law enforcement officer and she'd heard far worse. Ray was an old school gentleman about sex. She said, "I didn't know."

"I did. The investigation was eventually

stopped because the complainant was deemed unreliable. Ex-hooker, drug user, etc. But . . . I don't know. By statute, if a parole officer pressures an offender for sex, it's rape."

"Did you think he did it?"

"I thought he did, yeah. He was not a good man."

"Ray, you're not just saying this to make me feel better, are you? I mean, I'm feeling pretty low about what happened."

"Well, don't. I know you and I knew him and I'm sure it was a clean shoot. Listen, I think they know they've got a weak disciplinary case against you anyway."

"How come?"

"Because I was talking with Amy, your ADS, and she said she hoped they would get the investigation wrapped up soon, because now they've got to divide up Marlon's files too. On top of Seth's."

Chris said, "So let me get this straight: I'll be cleared because they need the manpower?"

Ray laughed. "That might be the case. Amy sure as hell doesn't want to do home visits."

"Thanks, Ray. I feel better now."

"I'll be in touch."

They said goodbye. Chris had always liked

Ray. He was good with words, good at taking care of people he thought were being mistreated. Maybe everything would be all right. She wanted to believe it. But Ray had a way of putting things in their best light; you could shine up a turd and put it in good light and it would still be a turd. If she was cleared, she would go back to work and they might punish her by doubling her workload and then coming after her for not keeping up. If she went back, she'd be handling Seth's files and Marlon's. How was that for irony?

Marlon.

Marlon had taken eleven of Seth's files and she had taken nine. Why had Marlon got more than her? One more.

She picked up the phone.

"Ray? . . . Yeah, it's me again . . . No, I'm all right. Listen, would you do me a favor? I'm not supposed to contact anyone at my office until the internal investigation is finished. But I need to know something . . ."

Bridger parallel parked the Ford in a spot behind an SUV. He shut down the engine and waited. Twelve minutes later, he looked in the passenger-side mirror and unlocked the doors. Chris Rider got in the passenger side. She wore jeans and a sweater and a short raincoat. She looked more feminine today. Bridger thought maybe it was because she wasn't on duty.

Chris said, "You have any trouble getting here?"

"No. I'm learning my way around the city."

"That's probably something you're good at," she said. Bridger didn't respond to that. Chris took a note pad out of her pocket. She said, "You ready?"

"Yeah."

"The offender's name is Eduardo Ramos. He was one of Seth's. After he was killed, he was supposed to be reassigned to me. But Marlon told our ADS he would take it. He told her it was to help me out. That's what got me wondering."

"When did you find this out?"

"Today." Chris looked at him, like he would have some kind of nerve distrusting her now. She said, "I wondered why Marlon would do that. Why he would take this one away? So I looked into it. His file states that he goes by Eddie Ramos. In his early thirties and he's spent most of his adulthood in and out of institutions."

"For what?"

"Armed robbery, assault and battery, unlawful possession of a firearm, breaking and entering. It goes back to juvie, which I don't have access to. Seven years ago, he was arrested and charged with murder. Before trial, the case started to fall apart. One witness retracted his story and the other was killed by an unknown assailant. The District Attorney had no doubt Ramos had killed one witness and threatened the other, but they had no evidence. They threatened to proceed with the trial. In a pretrial hearing, the judge ruled that the prosecutors could tell the jury that one of the witnesses was 'missing' and would let them draw their own conclusions. After that, both sides agreed to let Ramos plead to second-degree manslaughter. The judge accepted the plea and Ramos went to the state penitentiary. Served five years and was released on parole. That's when he came under Seth's supervision."

Bridger said, "I did more time than that."

"What an injustice," Chris said.

"Did Seth ever say anything about him?"

"Not really. Ramos would hardly have been the first shitbird he had to supervise. Seth didn't bother hating people, but he was no idealist."

"What's special about him?"

"Well, we can't ask Marlon, can we?" Chris looked at him, deadpan. She said,

"So, I made a few calls. There's some talk at Seattle PD that Ramos got involved in narcotics while he was in prison. That's not unusual, by the way. Guys go into prison for dumb shit, like armed robbery and then they find out how much more money can be made dealing drugs."

"I know that," Bridger said.

"Yeah, I'm sure you do. But . . . that's speculation. We have no solid evidence that Ramos is dealing now."

"Did Seth?"

"I don't know. I know if Seth had found drugs or guns on Ramos, he would have arrested him and filed an application to revoke his parole. With someone like that, a killer, Seth would not have given him a break."

Bridger said, "Maybe I should talk with this man."

"No," Chris said. "What we should do is report this information to the police. Tell the detective handling the case."

"He won't listen to me. Or you."

"You don't know that. Besides, what good do you think it's going to do, you 'talking' to him?"

"Because if I tell Detective Wilkening, the best that can happen is that he questions Ramos. If we're lucky, maybe he'll even arrest him and I don't think we'll be that lucky. But Wilkening's not going to look into the connection with Gage or Coates or any of those other guys."

"Maybe he will."

"He won't."

Bridger started the car, letting her know he was through discussing it. He put his hand on the gear lever, stopped and looked over at her.

Bridger said, "You can give me his address. If you don't, I'll find it on my own."

"I can't talk you out of this?"

Bridger said, "I'm just going to talk to him."

"Then I'll go with you," she said.

Eatherly and Dupree watched the lady back her car out of her driveway. They waited for her to get a few yards on them before they started following her. Dupree told Eatherly not to get too close and Eatherly told him he knew what the fuck he was doing. Eatherly had been a cop longer than Dupree and he didn't need that shit.

Eatherly kept cars between his Charger and Chris Rider's personal vehicle. They were tailing her because Dean had told them too. Dean said that was how they had almost got the man before. Marlon had followed the lady and she had led them right to Bridger. It was just that things didn't go right after that. Marlon should've popped the man right there in the parking lot. Found a way to explain it later. There was always a way to explain it. Dean had done it. The punk ass gangster had walked up to Dean's car and talked shit to him and started beating on him and Dean took the gun out and just did him right there. Found a way to deal with it *after.* The brass had tried to come after Dean later but Dean and Jim Patterson told them, "We were there, man, and you weren't. Who's gonna say different?" No one. Gage could have tried the same thing, but he had waited and look what it cost him.

Eatherly didn't miss Gage. He had never liked him anyway. Like many cops, Eatherly was a snob who looked down on probation officers. He didn't like having someone outside of their unit being involved in this. It made him nervous.

This made him nervous too. Having a dangerous criminal loose, looking after them, roughing up Hammond and not leaving town. The police could threaten them with their internal investigations and disciplinary panels and raised eyebrows, but they could handle that. Dean was good at handling that. But a man like this Bridger, a criminal, he had nothing to lose.

Dupree asked, "Think we should call Dean?"

Eatherly shook his head. "She's probably just going to the grocery store." Eatherly thought this was a shit detail. He'd worked surveillance only a few times in his law enforcement career. He never liked it. He didn't have the patience for it. Watching and waiting, waiting and watching.

But they passed a grocery store and the lady kept going. Then she got onto the interstate and headed south. About fifteen minutes later they saw her park her car and get out and start walking. They drove past her, Dupree looking at her in the side mirror, reasonably confident she didn't know she had been followed. They kept going and turned around two blocks up and came back. Not seeing her at first, but then looking closer and finding her.

There. In the car with Bridger. *There,* sitting right next to him.

*Jesus.*

Dupree said, "Is that him?"

"It's him," Eatherly said. He drove back another block, turned the corner and then did an eighteen point turnaround and went back. When he rounded the corner he saw the blue Ford pull out of the space, the man leaving and taking the woman with him.

Dupree took his cell phone out. "I'm calling Dean," Dupree said.

Dean Coates was having dinner with his wife and kids, sitting at the table soliciting news from his children, what was going on at school and with their extracurriculars, correcting the son when he spoke too sharply to his mom or sister, Dean holding court. His wife updated him on other family matters, seeking approval from a man she loved and generally looked up to. Dean was king here.

His cell phone rang and he looked at the screen and he answered it. He shook his head in silent apology to his wife, answering the phone at the table.

Dupree said, "We got him."

*"Him?"* Coates said. He wouldn't say the name aloud.

"Yeah, Bridger. He's heading south on the interstate. But Dean, he's got the probation officer with him. What are we supposed to do?"

"Stay with him. Don't do anything with her there. I'm coming."

Bridger parked the car in front of a red brick three-story apartment house. The front entrance had a small stone lion head over the door. Air conditioning units came out of the side windows. Bridger shut off the car and turned to Chris.

He said, "I think it would be better if you stayed here."

"Why?"

"Because you don't want to lose your job."

"I've come this far, Dan."

"He might be dangerous."

"So might you," Chris said. "I'm not going to sit out here while you carry out a vendetta."

"I told you, I'm just going to talk to him. Will you stay here, please?"

She looked at him and then out the front window. Finally, she nodded.

The front door was open. Bridger heard a television set blaring through the thin walls. A faint smell of urine in the stairwell. A dumpy, rundown place. He walked quietly up the stairs. On the second floor he walked down the hall to the apartment at the end. At the door he hesitated, listening. Another television, this one on a different program than the one downstairs. A laugh track. Bridger turned the knob on the door. The door was not locked. He opened it a notch then pushed it a bit further and that was when the chain caught and pulled taut.

Bridger stepped back and kicked the door in.

He pulled the .45 out as he went in. In front of the television set in two chairs were two young Hispanics. A young skinny man and a chubby girl. The skinny man held a plate of food in front of him, the plastic white fork still in his hand. The girl stood up.

"Sit down," Bridger said. "I said, sit down."

She did and Bridger looked at the skinny guy. "You Eduardo?"

"No, man," the guy said. "I don't know who you talking about."

"You got some identification?"

"What?"

"Identification. A driver's license. Something with your name on it."

"Yeah."

"Then show it to me. Easy."

The young man slowly reached into his back pocket for his wallet. Bridger followed the motion with his pointed gun, keeping it on the young Hispanic.

The girl said, "Eduardo's not here. This is my brother."

Bridger stepped closer and took the driver's license away from the young man. The young man started to stand and Bridger pushed him back down in the chair.

The driver's license said his name was Manuel Emiliano. Bridger looked him over. He did not fit the description of Eduardo Ramos Bridger had been given. Still . . . there was something not right about him. The thin, overconfident way he smiled, maybe. He couldn't weigh more than a hundred and thirty, but guys like this could spring.

Bridger looked beyond them to a bedroom in the back. He said, "Anyone back there?"

"No," Manuel said. "Here, I'll show you."

Bridger almost smiled. "Will you, now?"

"Yeah. Come on."

Bridger thought it would be better to keep this one in sight. He said, "Okay, let's go."

The man stood up, still smiling. Like, what you got to be upset about? Bridger followed him back to the bedroom. The guy walked through the door and then cut to his left, fast. Bridger went after him.

By the time Bridger got in the room, the guy was opening a closet door, reaching in and Bridger closed the door on his body. Bridger put his shoulder into the door and his weight behind it, feeling the skinny man's body being squeezed. Manuel cried out and Bridger reached across the door and grabbed him by the hair and pulled him out. Bridger backhanded him with the .45, knocking him back against the bed. Bridger kept the .45 on him and stepped back into the closet. In the closet he found a twelve-gauge shotgun.

Bridger took the shotgun out. He looked at the man sprawled on the ground, blood coming down from his lip.

"Don't kill him."

Bridger turned to see the girl standing in the doorway.

Bridger said, "Why not? He was going to kill me."

"You came in here with a gun."

"I just want to see Eduardo."

"He's not here."

"Where is he?"

"Who are you?"

"Where is he?"

"He only comes here once in a while. This is the address he gives his parole officer. He used to come here more, but . . . I don't know."

Bridger said, "Why the weapons?"

The girl sort of shrugged. That was all he was going to get.

Bridger gestured to Manuel. "Is he really your brother?"

"Half-brother." She shrugged again. "He comes by sometimes. He's a little crazy."

The little man looked up at Bridger, smiling again, red blood on his teeth.

"Yeah, well," Bridger said. "I'm going to have to take this with me. I don't care to be shot in the back while I'm walking down the stairs."

The girl said, "You find Eduardo, tell him the DVD player don't work no more and we need a new one."

Bridger nodded and walked out.

He reached the bottom of the stairs and turned and looked out the front door. He saw the black Charger through the opening.

He stepped back. He put the .45 in his belt. He still held the shotgun. He turned around and walked out the back door.

Dupree and Eatherly approached the Ford. They walked up both sides of the car, their pistols drawn and pointed down. Dupree held it behind his back when he bent down and knocked on the window.

Chris turned to see him. She rolled down the window.

Dupree held up his shield.

"Police officer," Dupree said. "Step out of the car, please."

Chris got out. She wished she had brought her service weapon. But they had taken it away from her when she was placed on paid suspension. That was the policy. Now she was being taken by men with badges, men she hadn't seen before, but men she was reasonably sure had pursued her before after she shot and killed Marlon Gage.

Dupree took her by the arm. "This way," he said, leading her away from the Ford. She saw the other cop holding his gun by his side, looking at the front door of the apartment building, finding a place behind the car. A place from which to shoot.

Chris said, "Who are you guys?"

Eatherly said, "Get her out of here."

Chris began to struggle, pulling her arm out of Dupree's grip. Dupree holstered his weapon and used both hands to restrain her. Eatherly looked over at them, shook his head and started to walk over to help.

Bridger came around the corner of the apartment building. He saw the two men occupied with Chris, their backs to him. Chris almost yelling at them now. Bridger silently willed her not to turn around and see him, because there wouldn't be a better time.

Bridger stepped out into the street, raised the shotgun and blew a round of buckshot into the front tire of the Dodge Charger.

Racked the slide and put another one in

the chamber as the men turned around.

"Hold it," Bridger called out. Watching the men freeze in their tracks because it's not an easy thing to look at a shotgun being pointed at you.

"Throw those guns down," Bridger said. "Hurry up!"

Eatherly threw his out in the street first. Bridger then pointed the barrel on Dupree.

Dupree found that he was no longer holding the woman and she had stepped away from him. It occurred to him then that he should have put the woman in front of him as a shield. But it had happened so fast. The man not coming out through the front door like they expected. The man just suddenly there in the street, blasting rounds out of a shotgun.

"Throw it down," Bridger said.

That did it. Dupree took the gun out of his holster and tossed it into the street.

Dupree managed to say, "You're making a mistake."

"Get down in the street," Bridger said. "On your bellies."

They did so. Eatherly and then Dupree. Bridger kicked the guns under the Charger.

"Chris," Bridger said. "Get in the car and start it."

Chris got in the Ford and started it.

Bridger looked at the men on the ground. Then he looked at the Charger. He remembered it from before. The men in it chasing him and the girl, intending to kill them then and intending to kill them now. Bridger sent a blast into the windshield, blowing it apart. Racked the slide again and blew out the radiator.

He got in the Ford and Chris drove away, flooring it. Bridger looked at the back window as they left. The cops still on the ground when the Ford rounded the corner.

# THIRTY

Dean Coates pressed the accelerator down when Dupree told him where they were at. Dupree and Eatherly didn't understand the significance of the address, but Coates did. It was Eddie Ramos's address. Bridger had found out where Ramos lived. If Bridger found Ramos and killed him that would end the deal and they would all be out a lot of money. Even if Bridger didn't kill him, just maybe frightened him a little, then Ramos would know about Bridger and that could fuck up the deal too.

He didn't feel any better when he got there and saw Eatherly and Dupree standing by a car that had been blown to shit. A couple of patrol cars approaching too because someone had called 911. Coates stopped the car and jumped out and ran to his men. They would have to get their stories straight for the patrol officers. Coates would do most of the talking, even though he hadn't been there when it happened.

Chris washed her face and came out of the bathroom and it became real again. Daniel Bridger standing by the window with the .45 in his hand, pulling the curtain back to look at the parking lot. They had parked the Ford in the back lot — no one cruising through would see it, but he was looking out there anyway. The twelve-gauge shotgun was under the bed.

*Well,* Chris thought, *here you are. A fugitive.*

She said, "Are we okay?" Being sarcastic now, or trying to be.

Bridger let the curtain fall. "Yeah," he said. "Just checking."

Chris sat on the bed and looked at him.

She said, "Did you rent that car?"

"Yeah."

"In your own name?"

"Yeah."

"You know they're going to find it then. I'm sure they got the tag written down."

Bridger sat in the chair with the wooden frame and the fake yellow leather seat. He said, "We're not going to use it anymore."

"Oh, okay," Chris said. "We'll just steal one? Drive across the Midwest robbing banks and living above people's garages?"

"Excuse me?"

"Nothing. It was a reference to Bonnie and Clyde."

Bridger didn't say anything. And Chris said, "Didn't you see it?"

"What?"

"The movie."

"Was that the one where the guy couldn't make love to the woman?"

"Yeah, that was it. They got killed at the end. It was supposed to be romantic."

"I saw it," Bridger said. "Years ago. It wasn't very accurate."

Chris Rider looked at him for a moment. "How do you know that?"

"I read a book about them. They were losers, nothing romantic about them."

"You read a —"

Bridger smiled. "Yes, I can read."

"Sorry," she said. "You know, I've never for a moment thought you were dumb. You're primitive, in a way. Maybe even barbaric. But you're not dumb."

"Thanks."

"You're welcome."

Bridger walked over to her. He handed her the .45.

"Here."

She said, "Why are you giving me this?"

"You don't have a weapon. Not that I

276

think anyone's going to be busting in, but if they do . . ."

"What are you going to do?"

"Take a shower."

"What if I leave?"

"If you do, you do. I'm not going to keep you here."

"What do you *want* me to do?"

"I think it would be better if you stayed here for a while."

"Why?"

"Because those guys might go after you. After what you've seen."

Chris set the .45 on the nightstand. "You think I'm safer here."

"Yes."

"I'll probably lose my job."

Bridger said, "You can tell them you were abducted."

"By you," she said.

"Yeah."

"But you're leaving it up to me?"

"Of course." Bridger said, "What do you think I am?"

Chris didn't answer him. Instead, she looked at him and said, "You know what I'd like? I'd like you to *ask* me to stay."

Bridger looked at her for a while, their eyes meeting. She looked back at him in a way she never had before.

Bridger said, "You're not making any sense." He shook his head and walked off to the bathroom. He closed the bathroom door behind him. A minute or so later, Chris heard the shower running.

Chris Rider looked at the wall and then at the television set, which was not turned on. She looked at the remote control and sighed. She got off the bed and walked to the mirror outside the bathroom. She looked at herself in the mirror. She put the .45 on the counter next to the sink. Then she pulled her top off. She unbuttoned her jeans and pulled them off. Then took off her panties and bra. She opened the door and walked in and joined him in the shower.

# THIRTY-ONE

Coates said, "You did receive field training, yes?"

"Dean —"

"You received field training?"

"Yeah," Dupree said. "But —"

Coates said, "Do you remember the part about covering the back?"

Dupree said, "We got here and we saw the woman and I thought it would be best — I thought it would be better if we had her covered first. That's when he came out from behind."

"Not through the front door," Coates said.

"Well, no. He must have . . ."

"He must have come out the back and come up behind you," Coates said.

Eatherly said, "You told us not to do anything until you got here. You didn't want us to do her too."

Coates was reconsidering that now. They should have just done her and then him. It would have been tough to explain. But maybe they would think she had it coming, hanging around with a known criminal. What *was* she doing there, anyway? The police reports said that she had killed Gage, but that didn't seem right. A probation officer gunning down another probation officer. For what? A shitbird thief?

Coates sat behind the wheel of his Chevy Suburban. Dupree next to him, Eatherly in the back. Coates had had to do a lot of talking to the uniformed officers back at Ramos's apartment. Tell them that a couple of Latino gangsters had done a drive-by, taken shots at the Dodge Charger. "They knew it was an unmarked police car, apparently," Coates had said. One of the uniformed officers then suggested that the Latinos maybe suspected that they were members of a rival gang. Coates had to swallow that racist shit. *Two niggers in a black Charger? Yeah of course they would be mistaken for gangsters.* Yeah, Coates said, that was possible too, though he told the young white officer he doubted it. Punk.

But they got out of there before any plain-clothes detectives showed up. Which was the main thing. They had been lucky.

But all this shit coming down. His girl-friend going nuts on him, a crook messing

280

up his plans and where was Ramos? Why hadn't Ramos called? They were supposed to get the deal done sometime tomorrow. Where the fuck was Ramos?

Coates had a number for Ramos, but of course it didn't work. Like many midlevel dope dealers, Ramos changed cell phones almost daily. Ramos had said, effectively, don't call me, I'll call you. And he hadn't called yet.

It was making Coates crazy. Like the genie who at first promises to reward the man who sets him free but as centuries go by becomes so angry he makes a vow to kill the man instead. Coates wanted to kill Ramos for making him wait. Kill him for holding control over the situation. Coates liked to be the one in control.

It would be nice to get the two of them together. Bridger and Ramos. Put them both against a wall and shoot them in the head. But tell them first. Tell Ramos he wasn't the player he thought he was before putting a cap in him. Then, let Bridger know that he was the one who killed his punk ass brother. Maybe even tell him why.

Tell him that his brother was a fucking dumb ass and that's why he got killed. Though it was Ramos who started it. Ramos who called Coates and told him his

probation officer had found a marijuana
one-hitter in his bedroom during a home
visit. Ramos told the parole officer that the
grass wasn't his, but his girlfriend's brother's. But the parole officer didn't care and
told Ramos he was going to have to file an
application to revoke his parole. Which
would send Ramos back to prison and fuck
up the deal Coates had with him.

Coates told Ramos not to worry about it.
He would talk to the parole officer and get
it straightened out. Coates genuinely believed it would not be a problem.

He was wrong. He met Seth Bridger at a
burger shack and offered to buy his lunch.
The parole officer refused the four-dollar
offer of burger and fries and Coates thought,
*Here we go.*

Coates talked a lot of law enforcement
fraternity shit first, letting him know they
were both on the same team. The parole
officer nodded politely even when Coates
asked him why someone of his intelligence
and ability hadn't applied to the Seattle PD.
Coates said he would be glad to write a letter of recommendation. The parole officer
said he would appreciate that, but he wasn't
really interested in law enforcement as a
long-term career anymore. Coates said, he
could understand that, smiling, but not lik-

ing the answer at all. Not liking the man's cool attitude either. He had expected the parole officer to show him some deference, but he hadn't. He hadn't been disrespectful, but he hadn't been deferential either. It had surprised Coates. Most parole officers wanted to please the cops.

Coates had said, "About Ramos. I need to ask you a favor."

"What favor?" Seth Bridger said.

"He's a key informant in an operation my unit is conducting. I would appreciate it greatly if you would not file that application to revoke."

The parole officer said, "Why?"

Coates suppressed his anger. "Well, I just told you why."

The parole officer said, "Mr. Ramos violated the rules and conditions of his parole. I have a duty to report it. You're certainly free to make your request to the District Attorney's Office after the charges are filed."

"I'm not asking them," Coates said. "I'm asking you. *Before* any charges are filed."

"Sergeant, there's nothing I can do."

"Yeah, there is," Coates said. "Boy, do you know anything about real police work?"

"I know the rules and conditions of an offender's parole. Particularly this one."

"You don't know anything about what's necessary. I told you Ramos is my informant. Is there something else you need to know?"

"No, not really." The parole officer stood up and picked up his tray. That was when Coates realized the man was ending the conversation.

It was probably then that Coates decided he was going to kill him. It was not so much the refusal to cooperate, but the way he refused. *No, not really.* The fucking insolence. There was nothing else he needed to know. This conversation was over. A total lack of respect from a punk, nobody, going nowhere parole officer.

Coates then said, "You're fucking up."

"I doubt it," the parole officer said. "If you've got a complaint, file it with my district supervisor." The parole officer's tone still nonchalant, almost bored. The parole officer put his tray on top of the trash receptacle and walked out.

Coates killed him the next day. Thought, *File that, bitch,* after it was done. He took the notebook off the parole officer to see if there were any notes about their conversation. There wasn't.

If he had known the man had a brother, a brother who was a hard-assed ex-convict,

284

would he have done the same thing? Fuck, yes, he would have. Then he would have flown out to Baltimore and killed the brother too. Or waited for him to step off the plane and capped him there.

It should be easier to do the brother. The brother was a criminal with a history of killing people. Shooting a known criminal would be an automatic clean shoot. The law enforcement community would be grateful that a police officer had taken a thief off the streets. Yeah, it should be easier . . . but the man was proving hard to kill.

Maybe he should have seen it coming. The parole officer didn't seem like much when Coates first saw him. A civil servant about a foot shorter than his brother, wearing one of those wimpy probation and parole satin jackets. A nobody. But the parole officer had stood up to him, had quietly and confidently held his ground. It had cost the parole officer his life. He had been stupid, but he had died brave.

Now Coates said, "You got a license number, right?"

"Yeah," Dupree said. "A car he rented from the airport. But it doesn't tell us where he is."

"What about his brother's apartment?"

"Hammond drove by there today, twice.

Checked the garage, too. He isn't there."

Coates said, "What about the girlfriend? Is she still there?"

"I don't know," Dupree said.

"Call him and find out."

# THIRTY-TWO

They lay in bed, Bridger on his back, Chris on her side facing him, her full breasts above the sheet, her knee draped over his leg. She said, "I haven't done that in a while."

Bridger said, "You haven't been with a man in a while?"

"No. Well, no, not for a while. But I meant in the shower. I thought I was getting too old for something like that."

"You're not old."

"I'm old*er*. About your age. But older than your brother. I didn't imagine this at all. Were you shocked when I came in?"

"I guess so."

"You warmed up quickly, I must say."

"It was good to see you."

"Had you thought about seeing me naked before that? Had you thought about me that way?"

"Sure."

"When?"

"The first time I met you."

"I like that. Does that make me slutty?"

"I don't think so."

"When you were in prison, what was that like?"

"Bad."

"Did you get raped?"

Bridger smiled. "What are you asking me something like that for?"

"I don't know. Just curious."

"No, I didn't get raped. It's not inevitable."

"Maybe you weren't pretty enough."

"Maybe. One guy tried something in the washroom. Or asked something. I don't remember all of it. I said no and he made a grab."

He didn't elaborate.

Chris said, "And what?"

"I bashed his head into the sink. He left me alone after that."

"I'll bet he did," Chris said. Thinking about her own grab for the keys in the shower. She said, "But you don't like hurting people, do you?"

"Are you asking me?"

"I was hoping I was making an observation."

"What I did then, I needed to do. And I

knew it would be better to do it in front of other people. In prison, you have to earn a reputation as soon as possible."

"To send a message to the other inmates?"

"You don't want to have to do something like that twice."

"No, I guess you don't." She said, "You know, I've sent people to prison. Or back to prison."

"Did you feel bad about it?"

It surprised her, him asking something like that. Two people in the dark, strangers but not strangers, having completed the most intimate of acts, now talking.

"I used to," she said. "You ever see that movie *Caddyshack*? There's a part in the movie when the judge says, 'I've sent boys younger than you to the gas chamber. I didn't want to do it, but I felt I *owed* it to them.' "

"That supposed to be the judge guy's voice?"

"Shut up." Chris said, "I always thought that was funny. But you know, they try to train us to think that way. We're putting these people away because we owe it to them. But that's not how it is. We're just moving them through the system, moving them out and moving them back in. We're supposed to think we're in the reforming business, but we're just sending them to a chamber, separating them from society."

"Not to die, though."

"No, not to die. But I know how bad prison is. I used to think about what bad things might happen to them once they got to prison. Especially the ones who didn't seem very strong. The ones who weren't hard core. The ones you knew would be victimized. And then . . . then one day I just stopped thinking about it. I told myself that they were the architects of their own demise."

"They usually are."

This surprised Chris too, in a way. But ex-cons who went straight were often some of the most conservative people you met. Chris said, "You think you deserved to be there?"

"Deserved? I guess so. I fucked up and got caught."

"That's a form of penitence, I suppose." She leaned up, crooked an elbow, and put her head on her hand. She said, "I want you to know I don't have a thing for dangerous men. I've never done anything like this before."

"I never thought you did." Bridger said, "Were you in love with Seth?"

Chris thought for a moment. She knew

the answer, but took time to formulate it. She said, "No. I loved him. You know, the way you can love someone you know and see everyday. And he was cute. But I wasn't pining for him or anything. I — wait, why are you asking me that?"

"Just asking."

"You don't think I did this to . . . to somehow make a connection with him, do you?"

"No."

"Because I didn't."

"Are you mad at me now?"

"No."

"You sure?"

"Yeah, I'm sure. Don't ask me about him anymore."

"All right."

A few moments passed. "Shit," Chris said. "I don't know what I'm getting upset for. I guess I feel a little guilty."

"For what?"

"I don't know. Enjoying it, I guess. I wonder what he'd think of me if he knew about this."

"Seth?"

"Yeah, Seth. Who did you think? It's not fair. He should be home in bed with *his* girl. He didn't deserve what happened to him. What was he, ten years younger than you?"

Bridger looked at the ceiling. "Yeah."

"A young man had his life ended, stolen from him. By who?"

"I think I know who."

"I think I do too. They were going to kill you. As soon as you came out that door, they were going to kill you. Kill Seth and then his brother and then probably me too. Shitbirds."

"They're police officers."

"They're gangsters, posing as police officers." She laughed to herself. "And you."

"What? Another gangster?"

"No, not a gangster. Not quite. A crook. Maybe there's a difference."

"Probably not much difference," Bridger said.

"Well, I'm going to have to believe there is. Because I need you now. I need you to get through this. And I'd like to think that maybe you need me."

"I do need you."

"Ah, what a sensitive fellow you are, confessing your deepest feelings." Her smile evaporated. She said, "He really was a good man, you know. I'm sorry you didn't know him better."

Bridger said, "I'm sorry too."

# THIRTY-THREE

Carnahan said, "You know where they got that car, don't you? Seized it in a drug raid, guy coming down the interstate on his way to San Francisco with a bunch of marijuana wrapped up in sandwich bags. I mean, in bags between *meat* wrapped in actual sandwiches. The runners thought the roast beef would throw the dogs off but they kept at it and smelled it anyway."

"I heard about that," Charney Harris said. "But never mind the dogs, Dean probably got a tip."

"But that's where they got the Charger. It's not police issue."

Harris said, "Yeah, and then when they got the car, Dean made a point of giving it to Eatherly. Like it was his to give. Elvis Presley, giving away Cadillacs."

"Yeah," Carnahan said, "but to see Eatherly drive it, you'd have thought he bought it with his own money. He called it *his* car.

These defense lawyers, they argue in court that the RICO act encourages police officers to steal because it gives the police a motive to bust people. And they kind of got a point."

"That's the law," Harris said. He picked up a piece of sesame chicken with his chopsticks and put it in his mouth. Carnahan had brought the Chinese food by the property room. Beef broccoli and white rice, chicken and fried rice. Harris hoped they didn't get the two mixed up.

Carnahan sat on the opposite side of the gray metal desk, his feet up, stabbing his fork into his box of moo goo gai-pan.

Harris said, "Still, I'd have loved to have seen the look on Eatherly's face when the car got massacred by a shotgun."

"Me, too," Carnahan said. "You think it was our boy?"

"I don't think it was Menudo, or whatever it was they told the patrol officers."

Carnahan said, "I could put a bug in my lieutenant's ear. Tell him maybe there needs to be an internal investigation on the incident. See if he'll carry it upstairs."

Harris shook his head. "Wouldn't do any good. Where are your witnesses? At best, you'd catch them lying in an investigation."

"Lying in an investigation's a termination

offense," Carnahan said.

"Even so, you have to prove it." Harris said, "They survive an IA, they'll come out stronger and then you'll be under the lamp. You told me that yourself."

"I was talking about you when I said that."

Harris shook his head again, poking around the rice on his plate for a hidden piece of chicken. He said, "They say they were hit by Latino gangsters, who's going to say they weren't?"

"Maybe one guy," Carnahan said. "If you can get him to come in."

"I don't want him coming in," Harris said. "Not yet."

She returned from the kitchen to hand the man a glass of ice water. He remained on the couch, not standing up when she walked back in the living room, remaining on the couch when she handed him the glass. It made her uncomfortable for some reason. A lack of manners perhaps. Or maybe he seemed too comfortable in her home when she had just met him. An attractive black man wearing a waist-length black leather jacket and a black T-shirt and expensive jeans. Well dressed and handsome, particularly for a police officer.

Elaine took a seat in the leather chair near

the couch. She said, "I'm not afraid of him."

Coates said, "You should be. The man is a criminal."

"He hasn't threatened me," Elaine said. "But there's been some . . . trouble, I guess. The other day, he looked like he had been in a fight."

"I'm not surprised," Coates said. "Did he say what it was about?"

"No."

"See," Coates said, "that's the thing. A man like that doesn't change."

"What has he done, exactly?"

"What he's done is assaulted a couple of police officers."

Coates had knocked on her door a few minutes ago and flashed her his badge and showed her his police identification. He had told her he wanted to ask her about Seth and Seth's brother. He said he had come to help.

Elaine said, "But why would he do that?"

The police officer seemed to think about it for a minute. Then he said, "Apparently, he was seen outside of someone's home, perhaps casing it for a robbery. He has a history of that, you know. He invades people's homes. You let him in this one?"

"I did," she said, not liking his tone. It was her home, hers and Seth's, and it was her business who she let in. "He didn't do anything wrong."

"But he has," Coates said. He shook his head, as if in sympathy. He said, "I know he's Seth's brother. And you're obviously a good girl. But the problem with nice people like yourself is you don't understand the convict mentality. They're called cons for a reason. What they're good at is convincing good people like yourself that they're misunderstood, that the system's always fucking them over. For example, I wouldn't be surprised if he told you the cops are trying to set him up."

"He hasn't told me that."

"He hasn't?"

"No. He just told me that Seth may have stumbled into something big and that that was why he was murdered."

Coates stared at her for a moment. A cop's stare . . . maybe. He said, "That's all he told you?"

"Yes."

"Do you know where he is now?"

"No."

"Now don't lie to me. He's not worth protecting."

"I'm not lying to you. I haven't seen him in a couple of days. In fact, the last time I saw him I asked him to leave me alone."

"Now there's a smart girl."

"I'm not a girl."

Dean Coates smiled. "Sorry. I meant lady."

Elaine Ogilvie did not smile back. She was beginning not to like this man. He was good-looking and he knew it, but he presumed a little too much. Maybe he meant well, but she didn't like the way he seemed to be coming on to her. Like she was at a club wearing a tube top. Seth had never behaved like this with her. Nor had his brother.

Coates said, "Do you know where he's staying?"

"No."

"Do you have a number for him?"

"No. He never gave me one."

Coates shook his head again. Like, *see what I'm talking about?* Elaine didn't like that either. Coates said, "That's not good. Did he ever tell you where he was staying?"

"No. He has my cell number though. Listen," Elaine said. "I don't much like him, but I seriously doubt he'd ever hurt me."

"I hope you're right," Coates said, "but he's been getting into some bad shit since he's been here. Why, I do not know. The way these guys are, sometimes they snap and they go on a crime spree. We want to find him before he hurts anyone else or gets himself hurt. We don't want any more violence. That's what you want too, isn't it?"

"Yes."

"So if you hear from him, I want you to call me. Okay?" Coates held his business card out and waited for her to take it. She eventually did, their fingers sharing the card for a moment. "That has my private cell number on it, okay? I want you to call me immediately as soon as you hear from him. Because we don't want any more trouble. Don't call 911. Just call me. I'll handle it from there."

He smiled at the woman again when she showed him out the door. Nice little piece. College, granola-type who didn't wear makeup; not his usual type, but maybe the sort who came alive in the bedroom. She was wary of him, he could see, but most people were wary of cops. Maybe when everything was finished and Bridger was put in the ground, he could come back and give her the good news. Tell her she had nothing more to worry her pretty little behind about and see if she'd like to go to lunch. It would be something different.

He got into his SUV and started it and his cell phone rang.

He hoped it would be Ramos. It was.

Coates said, "Where you been?" Putting a little edge in his tone, letting him know he didn't like to be kept waiting.

Eddie Ramos said, "I've been having to run around town." His voice was equally tense. And Coates had an idea why.

Ramos said, "I went by my place today, my lady told me some dude showed up there looking for me."

Coates said, "What are you talking about?"

"You tell me," Ramos said.

"Eddie, you're going to have to tell me what you're talking about."

"I'm talking about a mad motherfucker coming by my place looking for me. Taking my shotgun and shooting up a police car with it."

"Oh, that."

"Yeah, that."

"Eddie, let me ask you something. You been dealing on the side?"

"What?"

"You heard me," Coates said.

"What the fuck you talking about?"

"We don't hear from you for a while, we get nervous. So I sent a couple of my boys by your place to make sure you're still around. Out comes some crazy white motherfucker with a shotgun."

"Yeah, that's what I been telling you."

"And I'm asking you," Coates said, "is the man working for you?"

"What?"

"Is he your bodyguard? And if so, what do you need one for?"

"Bodyguard? Man, what the fuck I need a bodyguard for?"

"That's what I just asked you."

Ramos said, "I don't know who the fucker was."

"You sure?" Coates said, pressing his voice.

"Yeah, I'm sure. I thought you knew him."

"Come on, Eddie," Coates said. "I don't have any white guys on my crew." Coates waited, timing it. He said, "Well, I guess you got no reason to lie to me."

"I don't," Ramos said.

"Sorry for doubting you," Coates said. "Was the guy there to pick up something?"

"I told you, I'm not dealing."

"I'm not asking anymore," Coates said. "You see the man again, you should just shoot him. He's obviously crazy."

"Yeah," Ramos said. And Coates told himself it had passed.

Coates said, "Well, what's the status?"

"Meet me in a half hour. You know, where

we were last time. I'll tell you about it."

Coates asked, "Are you going to make me happy?"

"Don't I always?"

They met under the overpass, both men leaving their cell phones behind, leaning against their vehicles. Ramos was in a good mood, relaxed, his hands in his pockets. He said Aguilar was in town with his people and they were set up for the exchange tonight. One thirty A.M. Ramos smiling, probably because he would be getting some sort of finder's fee from Aguilar. That was okay with Coates. Eddie Ramos getting to feel big and rich for a few days until Coates would run him down and put a bullet in his head.

But that would come later. After the deal was done. Coates would feel better when he had the money.

# THIRTY-FOUR

Chris said, "Do you trust those guys?" She was referring to Carnahan and Harris.

Bridger said he didn't. He said the only one he trusted in this town was her. She thanked him kindly for that, and decided that he meant it.

Chris said, "I don't blame you. I wouldn't trust them either. But I guess what I meant was, do you believe them about Coates having stolen the ecstasy shipment?"

"That I believe," Bridger said. "I would have liked to have discussed it with Ramos. But now I've blown the opportunity. They're going to keep him hidden from me." Bridger put his coat on and leaned against the hotel room desk. Chris sat on the bed, fully dressed now. Both of them different, a little more guarded now that they were back in costume.

Chris said, "What are you thinking?"

"I'm thinking I should be following the

money."

"The money . . . ?"

"I mean, the product. If Coates stole that stuff, he's got it somewhere.

"If he hasn't moved it yet."

"You mean sold it," Chris said.

"Yeah."

"You have to be a little more specific for us people who aren't in the crime business."

Bridger looked at her, a little surprised.

"Sorry," Chris said, and she meant it.

"It's all right."

He wasn't thinking so much about her now. They had shared something nice, something they both needed, but now that it was done, he returned to his nature, which was precise and not especially warm. He realized she was aware of it, but he knew he was too old to change. What he was thinking about was the product. A shipment of stolen ecstasy, a dirty cop looking for a place to unload it. Getting rich after he'd killed Seth.

Carnahan and Harris . . . maybe they were dirty too. But Bridger kind of doubted it. They were using him and they probably wouldn't much care if he got killed so long as he pulled Coates and his crew down with him. But Bridger felt no personal animosity to Carnahan or Harris. Bridger had never wasted his time hating cops. He even felt a certain respect for men like Harris. They didn't talk smack and they didn't try to persuade you that you were anything more than a job to them.

Chris was a cop, too. Giving him more than he deserved, giving herself. It made him uncomfortable. He didn't want to need her, didn't want to pull her into this.

Now she was saying something.

"Pardon?"

Chris said, "If Coates has it, I doubt he'd keep it at his house."

"Yeah?"

Chris said, "I'm sure he's smart enough to know that Harris and Carnahan and maybe some other people in the department are watching him. They go to his home with a search warrant, they'd find it . . . maybe he's keeping it at one of those storage rental places."

"If so, it wouldn't be in his name."

"Maybe someone in his crew."

"No," Bridger said. "He wouldn't trust them."

Chris said, "They seem pretty loyal to him."

"He wouldn't trust them." Bridger looked at her. He said, "I need to check on something. Do you mind if I leave you here?"

"Yes."

"Well, then can I take you someplace?"

"You can take me home," Chris said.

"I don't like that idea."

"Well, it's not your choice, is it?" She looked back at him and sort of smiled. She was tough, all right. "Believe me, I can take care of myself."

"I believe that."

After he left Chris's house, Bridger drove back to the rental agency and switched cars. Turned in the blue Ford Crown Vic and drove out in a white Ford Mustang. He drove to the hotel and paged through the phonebook looking for Coates's number and address. There were two listings under D. Coates. One of them answered and told him it was the residence of David Coates. The other one did not answer. Bridger doubted that a police officer would list his number in the phonebook, but it was worth a try.

He took the shotgun out from under the bed and put it in the trunk of the Mustang. Then he drove to a pay phone and called the police department and asked for Coates. He waited for a while and eventually was transferred to a woman who told him Sergeant Coates was not in the office and was probably gone for the day. The secretary asked who it was. Bridger hung up.

Shit. He was calling the guy now. *Is Dean there? Do you know when he'll be back?* He didn't want to leave any messages. He wanted to find the guy. A cop named Dean Coates and another one named Michael Hammond and a few other guys he didn't have names for. They were looking for him now and they wanted to kill him. They would look in the hotel he had been staying in under his own name, looking at places where they'd hope he would be.

Oh, hell.

Bridger got back in the Mustang.

He arrived at Seth and Elaine's apartment about twenty minutes later. He circled the block and didn't see anything that made him too nervous. He parked the car and checked his coat to make sure the .45 was still there. Then he rang the doorbell.

Elaine stood at the top of the stairs looking down. She suspected it was him and then she turned the front porch light on and saw that it *was* him. Seeing him the same way she had seen him a few days ago, standing at the bottom of the stairs, the brother of the man she was going to marry, the man whose child she was carrying. Seeing Daniel Bridger, the man she had spoken to the first time to tell him his brother was dead.

She could call the police. She could call the cop who told her in no uncertain terms that he was to call her immediately when she saw Bridger again. A dangerous man, a criminal. That's what the police officer had said.

The cop's card with his number on it, resting on the coffee table where she had left it and after he had gone. She had left it there instead of putting it in a drawer, wanting to put it away because she had not liked the cop or his manners.

Now Bridger was looking at her through the window in the door. He had seen her and she knew it. What could she do?

She heard him through the glass, saying, "I need to talk to you. Please."

*Who do you trust?* Elaine looked down at him, not really caring that he saw her, not really caring what he thought of her. This criminal, this thief who did not know his own brother. At the other end, a police officer who smiled at her and hit on her and made her feel uncomfortable in her own home. A man saying, in effect, he was from the government and he was here to help. A cynical expression her father liked to use.

Her father was a businessman with politically conservative leanings who liked to say things like that, a man she didn't always see eye-to-eye with but whom she loved and respected. This ex-convict, was he family? Could she think of him as a relation? *What do I do about him, daddy?* The thief had not tried to persuade her to like him. He had not asked her to trust him. The last time she saw him, she had chewed him out and told him she didn't want to see him again, maybe because she was angry at him or maybe because she didn't like him or maybe because Seth was dead and he was still alive.

Elaine pressed the buzzer, releasing the lock on the door.

Bridger stepped in and closed the door behind him. For some reason, it made her feel better. Maybe because she had made the decision and she didn't have to think about it anymore.

But that didn't mean she had to be nice to him.

In an unfriendly voice, she said, "What do you want?"

Bridger said, "I think I know who killed Seth."

When he was in the apartment, she thought about telling him not to bother taking off his coat because he wouldn't be staying. But he didn't take off his coat anyway. He made no attempt to sit down or make himself comfortable. This too made her feel a little better. Elaine stood near him, did not step away from him. She looked him in the eye and said, "Tell me."

"I think he was killed by a cop."

She stared at him for a moment. A connection formed in her mind, brief, but too fantastic to contemplate. "What?"

"A police officer working in narcotics. A crooked cop. It had something to do with an offender Seth was watching. It's hard to explain."

Her voice firm, Elaine said, "Try."

"The other day, when I looked like I'd been in a fight, it was done by two off-duty cops. One of them was named Michael Hammond. He's working for another cop, a guy named Coates. They stole some ecstasy and they're trying to sell it. I guess Seth got in the way of the deal."

Elaine said, "Did you say Coates?"

"Yeah."

She walked over to the table and picked up the card and brought it back to him.

Bridger took the card and read it. "Where did you get this?"

"He was here. He told me to call him as

soon as I saw you."

Bridger gave her a long look. Then he said, "Well, do you want to call him?"

"What are you asking me that for?" Elaine said. "Do you want me to take his word over yours?"

"I want to know what you believe."

"I don't *know*."

"He killed Seth. You want to know how *I* know that? A couple of other cops told me he did."

"I don't understand. If the police know it, why don't they arrest him?"

"Because they don't have any evidence he did. They told me because they want me to do something about it. Clean up a mess for them within the police department."

"And what about Seth?"

"They don't care about Seth. Any of them."

"Coates said you were dangerous. He said you were on a crime spree. That you were unstable."

"Did Seth ever tell you I was unstable?"

". . . no."

"What do you think?"

"I think you're a lot of things, but not unstable."

"All right. Now what do you think of Coates? Quick now."

"I didn't like him. But that doesn't mean —"

"Why didn't you like him?"

"I don't know. He came on to me. He was just a little too smooth. But I hear a lot of cops will hit on you."

"Not all. Elaine, listen to me. I don't have direct proof that he killed Seth. But I know it. It all pieces together. If he has drugs in his possession, drugs he's trying to sell through the man Seth was assigned to, it all fits. Trust me on this: I know how criminals think. And Dean Coates is a criminal."

She looked around the room. She looked at the couch where he had been sitting, remembered how she didn't want to sit next to him. Remembered the way he had looked into her eyes, trying to make a connection with her. Then she remembered something else.

Elaine said, "He said if I saw you, I was supposed to call him. Not 911 . . . I don't know. Maybe it means something."

Bridger said, "Do you have a friend you can stay with? I mean, tonight."

"I think so."

"Set it up. I'll take you there."

Elaine thought of something. She faltered and had to sit down. "Oh, God," she said. "If you're right, he — God, he was trying to

312

seduce me. After what he did . . ."

"Forget about that," Bridger said. "We have to get out of here."

Bridger dropped Elaine off at her friend's, walked her in and said goodbye. As he drove away he thought of Dean Coates hitting on Elaine, his brother's girl, sitting there and smiling at her after he'd put the father of her child in the grave. He thought of the shotgun in his trunk and how badly he wanted to use it. Track the fucker down and blow a hole through his chest. No. Put the barrel in his face, under his nose, and say to him, "You tell me what happened." And if Coates was scared, he would tell. He would confess.

But this was no chickenshit small-timer. This was a bold man. Maybe he'd look back at Bridger and say, "I don't know what you're talking about." Say it in his confident, no-shame, gangster tone. Tell Bridger he could pull the trigger but it wouldn't change anything. Maybe he'd even tell Bridger he was in big trouble, pointing a weapon at a cop.

The thing was, he didn't know. The man was a stranger to him. Someone he knew about, someone whose picture he had seen. But someone he had never seen or had an opportunity to size up.

Bridger pulled the car over and took the card out of his pocket. Looked at the number and made the call.

Three rings and he was wondering what sort of message he would leave. But the man answered on the fourth ring.

"Hello."

"Sergeant Coates?"

"Yeah. Who am I speaking to?"

"Daniel Bridger."

A pause. Then a voice saying, "No shit. For real?"

"For real. I understand you may be looking for me."

"Why's that?" Coates said. Bridger could hear the smile in his voice.

"I don't know," Bridger said. "Perhaps there's been a misunderstanding. Maybe we should get together and talk, clear it up."

"Yeah, maybe. How did you get this number?"

"Your friend Hammond gave it to me."

"Michael? No, he wouldn't have done that."

"He did."

Coates laughed. "You're a pretty smart fella, trying to get us to turn against each other. Rather amateurish move for a man I heard was a professional."

"You asked me a question," Bridger said. "I answered it."

"Well," Coates said. "I guess you figured it was worth a try. What I'm wondering is, what do we have to talk about?"

"My brother."

"I understand he was killed. I'm real sorry."

"Yeah, it was a tragedy."

"It's always tragic when a brother officer gets killed," Coates said. "But respectfully, I don't see what it has to do with me."

"No," Bridger said. "I don't suppose you would. Well, maybe we can talk about that load of ecstasy you stole."

A silence. Bridger waited. Both of them aware that they were discussing such things on a cell phone.

Coates sensed he was losing control of the conversation. He wondered, *How? How could the man know?* But Coates had had plenty of experience dealing with tight situations from his days in narcotics and he was a natural actor, quick on his feet. He laughed again and said, "Man, what are you on? That's some crazy shit you're saying."

Bridger said, "Gage told me. I guess he figured he'd tell me since he thought I was going to die anyway."

"Well, that's interesting," Coates said.

"Yes, it is. Anyway," Bridger said. "I'm going to be at the Blue Rose bowling alley in two hours. Come alone." He hung up before Coates could say anything else.

# THIRTY-FIVE

He picked up a pair of binoculars at a sporting goods store. From there, he drove to a convenience store. He bought a Coca-Cola in a glass bottle and a yellow T-shirt that said he loved Seattle. He took a couple of sips of the soda, then poured the rest of it on the ground while he pumped gas into the Mustang.

From the convenience store, he drove to the bowling alley. The bowling alley was on a stretch of four-lane road in a rundown commercial area. Bridger drove past the bowling alley and made a right turn at the next block. He turned into a lot behind a used-car dealership and parked the Mustang there. He considered the shotgun in the trunk but decided to leave it there. He still had the .45. He walked down an alley and came to an area closed off by a wood fence. He looked through a crack and saw some shabby, third-hand cars with prices written wide on the windshield. No one would steal them. A wood fence above his head, but at least it wasn't chain link with barbed wire on top. He hadn't brought any tools for that sort of thing.

He wrapped the binocular strap around his neck and shoulder and jumped up to grab the top of the fence. He pulled himself over.

Now he was in the lot. Through the rusted SUVs and cars he could see the bowling alley across the street, pink walls with a neon blue rose on top. He moved back behind the building that housed the offices of the car dealership. It was a one-story building with chalk-white sides. There was a dumpster at the back of the lot near the fence. He could push that over to the back of the building but that would make a lot of noise. But there was a yellow and red Chevy van with a big space in the side where the window had been knocked out — an ice cream truck. It seemed close enough.

Bridger climbed on top of the van and found that when he reached he could place his hands on top of the roof. He jumped and grabbed and pulled himself up. He was on a black tar roof. He stood for a moment, taking things in. The bowling alley parking lot to the right of the bowling alley. Bridger crouched then got on his stomach. He crawled forward to the front of the building. He was an hour early but there was no sense in taking chances. Coates and his crew could be in the parking lot already, maybe with a man with a high-powered rifle. Bridger got comfortable and waited.

Eighteen minutes later, he saw a dark Monte Carlo pull into the lot. Two guys got out and when they walked to the entrance Bridger saw that they were black. He raised the binoculars to his eyes. Panned left to right. His two old friends — Patterson and Hammond. Patterson said something to Hammond and Hammond went back to the parking lot.

*Covering the back door,* Bridger thought.

Patterson went in alone. A few minutes later, two more men showed up. Eatherly and Dupree, driving a different car than the Charger Bridger had destroyed. They went inside too.

Coates came last, driving a black Chevy Suburban with the Denali sport package.

Bridger watched him with the binoculars. The man had a confident walk, crossing through the parking lot with long even strides, looking good in his black leather jacket and black shirt and boots. Bridger reached inside his coat pocket and touched his gun. Coates coming closer now, getting under the lights of the bowling alley entrance and Bridger saw his facial features through the binoculars. The same man he had seen in a photograph.

Coates hesitated at the entrance, did a quick look at the street. A cop's scan. Bridger pressed himself into the roof. *He can't see you at this distance,* he thought. *Not in the dark.* But then maybe he could if he knew where to look.

But then Coates went inside.

Another half hour or so until they were supposed to meet.

Bridger lowered the binoculars. He relaxed, a little.

Relaxed and took time to think. Thinking, what would you do anyway? Go in there with your little .45 and . . . what? Start shooting at black guys?

The good: there was no sign of uniformed police officers. If they were clean, they would have called in a tactical team, police officers with uniforms and hats and Oakley sunglasses who liked opportunities to shoot people. Standard police procedure was to call in tactical when dealing with a known criminal who was armed and dangerous. Sensible way to deal with a man who had blown apart an unmarked police car with a shotgun. But there were no police cars, no signs of a legitimate takedown. Which meant he wouldn't have to worry about a police helicopter shining a spotlight on him while he was on the roof. They weren't calling in patrol units because they weren't clean. They were rogue cops looking for a man they wanted to kill.

The bad: five guys. One outside and four in. Coates wasn't going to host any sort of fair fight. If he was smart — and he probably was — he would have his crew positioned around the bowling alley. Bridger could walk in, move a few steps, and have one of them step behind him and put a bullet in his back and then another couple in his head just to make sure. Claim self-defense because, after all, the man had a .45 on him. Maybe he could sneak around and go through the back and somehow get the jump on Coates that way. But then they had posted a man in the back and even if Bridger got past him, Coates probably had another man in the back inside.

*You asked him to come and now he's here. You can go down there and get it done, but there would be no way you would come out of it alive.* And Coates probably would.

Coates sat at a table nursing a tall glass of

Pabst Blue Ribbon. Patterson sat on the opposite side of him. Patterson was a big man, broad across the back. If Bridger came in the front door, Patterson would be between them.

They were in the dining area, a level above the lanes. Bowling balls crashing against pins, maybe once in a while a small cheer arising from someone who'd bowled a strike or got a spare that seemed impossibly split. Behind the service counter, a flat-screen television showed a basketball game between the Sixers and the team that used to play in Seattle. The sound of the game muted so the patrons could hear Steve Perry singing "Don't Stop Believing" over the alley's loudspeakers.

Dupree was posted near the back door. Eatherly sat on the level below at one of the bowling stands that wasn't being used, holding a sawed-off shotgun under his long coat.

Coates looked at the red menu encased in plastic, a lot of bad, fatty food, but priced cheap. Cheeseburger basket, fries, and a drink for $5.95. Downtown it would cost you at least twenty bucks, excluding the price of your bottled water. He wondered how Tulie would react if he brought her here.

Coates said, "You hungry?"

Patterson glanced across the table at him. Look at Dean. Trying to act cool, sipping his beer and looking at the menu. Patterson said, "Maybe when we're finished."

Coates said, "It'll happen when it'll happen. No need to be anxious."

"Right," Patterson said, smiling to himself. Patterson held a long-barreled .357 revolver under his jacket. He had never put a lot of stock in semiautomatics. They said the newer models never jammed, but why take a chance? Dean had said to him earlier, let's see what the man has to say. Then we do him. Patterson said, yeah, that was all nice, but a perp will do what he wants, not what you want and it was better to shoot first and ask questions later. The dog that fights and wins just goes straight to it and dispenses with the foreplay.

Now Coates said, "Everything's been checked?" Trying to be casual about it.

Patterson said, "Yeah. Bathrooms, back rooms, service areas. Everything. He's not here waiting. I already told you."

"Just making sure."

"Okay," Patterson said, "But do you really think he's coming here?"

"Why wouldn't he?"

"Because he knows it's stupid."

Coates said, "He said come alone. He's

not expecting me to bring backup."

"Yeah, he is. I told you before, the man's not dumb."

"What are we supposed to do? We need to find the man. Are we supposed to pass up an opportunity to pop him?"

"It feels all wrong," Patterson said. "He told you where you were going to meet him. You let him set the terms because you want him so bad."

"He needs to die."

"Time and a place, brother. This isn't the time or the place."

Coates said, "You afraid of him?"

"Let's just say I'm wary of him because I have reason to be." Patterson leaned back. "But that's not where I'm coming from."

"You tell me where you're coming from."

Patterson said, "We've got important business to take care of. In about three hours."

"We'll get to that," Coates said.

"We got a shooting here, homicide's going to be called in and question everybody and I mean everybody. We'll be here all night. The *cholos* may not grant us a second meeting."

"Yeah they will," Coates said. "We have what they want."

"Dean, have you ever dealt with Aguilar before? He's one of the top men in the Los

Cholos. Do you know what the Los Cholos cartel is? How big they are? The man Aguilar works for is on the *Forbes* list of the richest people in the world. His fortune's bigger than Campbell's Soup. They *own* most of northern Mexico. These guys, you show them disrespect, they put you in a trash barrel filled with gasoline and set you on fire and *laugh*. These are not the kind of people you reschedule with. They're criminals."

"They're a criminal *enterprise*. A billion-dollar enterprise. They're not northside crips working a corner."

"I understand that."

"You sure?" Coates glared at him, but he went on. "Because I think your priorities are a little mixed up. I want this finished. Tonight. Now are you on the team or not?"

"Well, which team is it? Special Investigations? Or the dope dealer team? Or is it the assassin squad? Which is it, Dean?"

"I never heard you complain before, brother. You took your share just like the rest of us. You think I'm a shitbird? Well, you were there with me all along."

"Yeah, I did. And I'm accountable for it. But what you did to the parole officer . . ."

"It had to be done," Coates said.

"I didn't want that."

"You want the same things I want. You

325

want to be in charge? You want this respon-
sibility? If not, you need to shut the fuck
up. I made a decision that benefits all of us.
*I* did it. Now it seems to me you want it
both ways. The money and the clothes and
the good life, but let old Dean do the dirty
shit while you sit there in judgment. I'll tell
you, I expected better from a friend."

There was a silence between them. Coates
staring at Patterson, though not staring him
down.

And then Patterson said, "You got a point.
But hear me out on one thing. Let's leave
this place and finish our business with the
Cholos. Let's seal that deal. Fucking forget
Bridger. Leave him for another time. He'll
leave town and if he doesn't we'll get him
later. Forget him for tonight."

"Your suggestion has been considered and
rejected," Coates said. "Now are you going
to take your post by the front, or do I have
to ask Charles to do it?"

Patterson left the table and walked down
to the bowling stands by the lanes. To the
front where he took his place to wait for the
man they would kill.

At ten minutes past the expected time,
Coates called Hammond in the parking lot
and asked him if he'd seen anything. Ham-

mond said he saw cars come and go but no sign of their man. At twelve minutes past, Coates ordered another beer. At thirty minutes past, he got up from the table and walked toward the entrance, glancing at Patterson as he went by, Patterson making a gesture of helplessness. Coates walked back to his table, looked at the television for a while and his empty beer glass. He went to the bathroom and came out and almost went to the bar to order another one, but told himself it was a bad idea. At fifty minutes past, he started to think about Ramos and the Cholos and the place he had stored the ecstasy. He wished it was in the Suburban so he could go straight to the meeting place but it wasn't and he had to move, now.

He gathered his men at the table. He said, "One of us has to stay here, in case he comes."

There was an uncomfortable silence. Hammond glancing at the others, Eatherly looking at Dupree but not at Coates.

Patterson said, "I don't think he's coming here."

"Well, what if he does?" Coates said, his voice raised. The men looking at him now, seeing him rattled.

Eatherly finally said, "Alex and I can stay."

"No," Coates said. He was meeting with Eduardo Aguilar, a lieutenant with the Cholos, and he was expecting Aguilar to bring a lot of muscle, heavily armed. He wanted as many men as possible around him. "Only one of you should stay."

"Dean," Patterson said. "If you want me to, I'll stay."

Coates regarded Patterson. His friend and the toughest one among them. But Patterson had second-guessed him and Coates wasn't going to forget that. He didn't trust Patterson anymore. Would Patterson kill the man like he had said he would? Or would he walk away from this whole thing?

Coates looked at Eatherly and said, "Charles, you stay. You see him, kill him. We'll back you up."

Eatherly looked back at Coates, wondering just how they could back him up if they weren't here. It didn't seem that well thought out. He wanted another man to stay with him. But he nodded and said, "Okay."

Coates looked at his watch. They had an hour and ten minutes to meet Aguilar and Ramos. It would probably be enough time to pick up the ecstasy and get there, but he wasn't sure.

Coates said, "Jim, you and Alex go to the Green Hills Motel. There'll be a room with a red SUV parked in front of it. That's the room where we're supposed to meet Aguilar. If we're not there by one thirty, tell Aguilar we'll be there soon. Stall him, tell him you're sorry, *anything,* but keep him there. Michael, you come with me."

# Thirty-Six

He had never told Hammond where he had been storing the ecstasy. He had never told any of his crew where he had put it. It wasn't easy, keeping quiet about it. They had been with him when they busted into the cabin near the Canadian border, wearing ski masks and holding shotguns, using a tip he had received from one of his many informants. Two granola guys with long hair and shorts and T-shirts who looked like they were about nineteen years old, smoking weed and watching television when five armed men came in and put them on the floor face down and told them they were gonna die if they didn't say where they were keeping the tabs. Coates was the only one who did the talking; he had told the others not to say anything unless absolutely necessary. Coates squatted down next to one of the boys and put a hand on his shoulder and said, "Just tell us, huh? And then we'll leave. It's better than having a bullet in your brain."

It was the other boy who said it was in the bedroom. Coates signaled to Patterson and Eatherly, heard a "fuck, yeah" a few moments later. They brought out two cardboard boxes, two by three, filled with sandwich bags containing ecstasy pills. Light enough for one man to lift. They carried the boxes out to their vehicles while Coates stroked the boy's hair and told him he had done good. They tied the boys up and gagged them and put them in the bedroom closet and took their cell phones away.

Got back to Seattle and Coates thought, was it really that easy? No armed guards, no fence, no hard-hitting homeboys standing at the door. Just a couple of white stoners in possession of millions of dollars' worth of little pills. Like walking in a bank where everyone had gone home and left the vault door open.

The thing was, Coates had known where it was and when it would be there. Information *was* power. He wished he had learned that lesson earlier in his life, but now he did know and he had plenty of years left in him and plenty more opportunities.

When they returned to Seattle, he worried that a *Treasure of Sierra Madre* effect would

331

descend upon his crew, men getting greedy, suspecting him of wanting to keep it all. But it didn't happen. He dropped the men off and told them he would store the pills and set up a deal soon and then they would split the money. No one objected, not even Patterson or Dupree, who had always over-estimated his intelligence. Maybe it would have been different if they had stolen two boxes filled with cash, which you could see and touch and imagine stuffing in your pockets. Still, they knew it was something of value. Already, Coates had overheard Dupree talking about a new boat he had his eye on.

At first, he had considered storing it at Tulie's apartment. But then he thought better of it and opened up an account at a storage facility in her name. She had to go with him to the Twin Oaks Storage facility and fill out the paperwork, but only Coates had the key to the combination lock.

Now he and Hammond pulled up to the iron gate of Twin Oaks Storage. Coates leaned out the window and punched in the code. The black iron gate slid open and Coates drove the Suburban through.

It was a big facility, covering as much space as a football field. Rows upon rows of taupe-colored units, varying in size, with red panel doors. On the sides of the facility were a few boats resting on trailers.

Hammond said, "You kept it here?" There was a dubious tone in his voice, like maybe they should have kept three million dollars' worth of ecstasy in a more secure place.

Coates said, "Couldn't very well put it in a safety deposit box. Or my garage."

"I know, but . . ."

"It's just boxes," Coates said. "No one knew it was here, except me."

Coates drove down the length of the facility, made a left turn at the end, went past four rows, then made another left. He went about a third of the way down that row and stopped. He cut the engine and got out. He pulled a key from his pocket and unlocked the door to a small walk-in unit.

The first thing he saw was an unstained night table. It had been in his basement. He brought it here so that the boxes wouldn't be the only things in the storage unit. He also put in some old books and clothes and some chairs Tulie was going to throw out after he had bought her some new ones. Yes, the boxes needed some company, make things look nice and natural.

He took his police flashlight and beamed it inside. There they were, at the back. He suppressed a smile. There was no logical way that someone could have come in here and replaced the boxes or taken out the tabs and put in bags of colored navy beans. But he would feel better when he checked.

He opened the first box and went through it.

From the door, Michael speaking. "Dean?"

Now the second box.

"Dean. Is everything okay?"

"Yeah," Coates said, and now he smiled. "Yeah, everything's fine."

Hammond helped him load the boxes into the Suburban. Coates got back behind the wheel and they moved forward, the headlights illuminating the white brick wall of the facility, pushing up as they reached the end of the row and made the tight turn that would bring them to the exit.

They made another right turn and waited for the underground magnetic sensor to open the gate and let them out. Counted to three.

But the gate didn't open.

They waited a couple more seconds. The gate stayed shut. Hammond looked over to Coates, saw the cool demeanor begin to slack.

"Dean —"

Both of them wondering in that moment

if someone had jacked with the gate —

The back door of the Suburban opened. It triggered the interior dome light. Hammond and Coates turned to see Bridger toss something in the back next to the boxes. A quick look at Bridger, right there, and then he shut the door and was gone.

They reached for their sidearms, Coates quicker than Hammond, Coates with his pistol out, extending it over the seat and blowing a hole through the rear window, the window shattering and Coates firing three more times, Hammond finally getting his pistol loose from his side holster and starting to aim because he didn't know if Coates had hit anything, but then Hammond looked at the little orange flame next to the boxes. A paper towel on fire . . . ?

No, not a paper towel. A torn yellow cloth sticking out of a bottle, filled with gasoline.

Hammond opened the door and jumped out as the bottle ignited and exploded, the back of the Suburban suddenly filled with flames.

Coates got out of his side, looked down the row of storage spaces, not seeing the man, but looking across the hood of the Suburban and seeing Hammond running full out to his right. And Coates said, "Hey!" Like he didn't want him to run away; he needed him to stay and put out this goddamn fire.

But the whole back of the vehicle was engulfed in flames, the cardboard boxes catching fire now, the boxes sitting above the gas tank —

Coates ran down the row, perpendicular to where Hammond had gone, not having time to run around the Suburban, but running straight and hard and then the gas tanks caught and the Suburban blew apart, sending bits of it up into the air, suspending for a moment before raining down on the ground.

The impact knocked Coates to the ground, threw him face flat, dropping his gun in the process.

Coates put himself on an elbow and looked back. Flames dancing up to the night sky, the vehicle now an opened, burning husk. He could feel the heat of it, hear the fire crackling.

He turned around and saw the man pointing a .45 at him.

Coates said, "You just cost me three million dollars."

Bridger said, "What about Seth?" He spoke softly, a quiet conversational tone. He was aware that the other man was still in the facility and he didn't want to be heard.

"He could have had a piece too," Coates said. "If he'd been smart and played along."

"Did you ask him?"

Coates shook his head. "Wouldn't have done any good. Guys like that don't know how to play." Coates eyed his pistol, on the ground about five feet in front of him. He could talk shit with this man, exploit his curiosity and upset his concentration. Where was Hammond?

Coates looked at Bridger and smiled and said, "Not like you and me, huh? We could have worked out a deal too. Maybe we still can. There's more where that came from."

He waited for Bridger to respond to that one. Maybe say something like, *I'm sure there is.*

But Bridger just shook his head and said, "You want to try it, go ahead. But I don't think you're quick enough."

Coates got his meaning, the man taunting him now, telling him he wouldn't be quick enough to get to the gun. And Coates got angry, looking beyond Bridger and saying, "Shoot him!" as if Hammond were there. And Bridger turned and looked, a reflex, and Coates rushed for the pistol and Bridger turned and shot him in the chest. Pulled the trigger two more times and shot Coates in the face and body. Coates slumped to the ground and Bridger shot him once more in the head.

Bridger looked up and down the row. He saw no sign of Hammond. He kicked Coates's pistol to the side and then used his foot to nudge Coates's body over on its back.

Bridger looked up the aisle to the flaming wreck and called out.

"Hammond! Your boss is dead and your product is gone. Your part in this is finished. Stay out of my way and I won't kill you. You hear me?"

Bridger waited a few moments before he started walking carefully up the side of the row. He got to the burning Suburban and looked around the corner. He didn't see Hammond. The explosion of the vehicle had knocked the gate off its hinges. He crawled through the open space and walked into the shadows. Before he reached his car, he heard the approaching sirens of the fire engines.

# THIRTY-SEVEN

The manager of the storage facility had opened his office after the fire department called him and told him there had been an explosion at his business. Now the manager was in the parking lot with about forty members of the police and fire departments. The fire was out now, but the smoke and smell still permeated the air. The manager sitting in the front room of his little wooden office that was built to look like a quaint log cabin, wondering how such a thing could have happened at his establishment.

Mitch Carnahan came in and said, "Hey, brother. You mind if I use your phone?"

The manager looked at him and thought, *Another one.* All these cops hanging around his business. City, state and now he was going to have to take questions from some federal guys who said they were from the DEA. What did *they* want? What had any of this to do with him?

"Don't you have a cell phone?"

"Sir, it's police business," Carnahan said, giving him that regretful but official tone he had mastered over the years. He didn't want to risk using the cell phone and having the conversation picked up on a scanner.

"Go ahead," the manager said, resigned to it.

Carnahan went to the private office in the back and shut the door. He looked at a calendar on the wall with a picture of a little barn somewhere in the deep snow of New England. A smile on his face as he dialed the number.

Charney Harris answered. "Yeah."

"Wake up, sunshine," Carnahan said. "Coates is dead. And you'll never guess what they found in the charred remains of his vehicle."

"I got a good idea," Harris said. "Who's left?"

"He's the only one who was killed. They're rounding the rest up now. I'm told they'll initiate an internal investigation in the morning and a criminal one is in the pipe. I predict Eatherly will be the first one to crack."

"I say Dupree," Harris said. "If I'm wrong, I'll buy you a Coke."

Carnahan said, "Let the games begin."

# ABOUT THE AUTHOR

**James Patrick Hunt** was born in Surrey, England, in 1964. He graduated from Parks College of Saint Louis University with a degree in aerospace engineering in 1986 and from Marquette University Law School in 1992. He resides in Tulsa, Oklahoma, where he writes and practices law. He is the author of *Maitland, Maitland Under Siege, Before They Make You Run, The Betrayers, Goodbye Sister Disco, The Assailant, Maitland's Reply, The Silent Places, Bridger,* and *Get Maitland.*

The Employees of Thorndike Press hope you have enjoyed this Large Print book. All our Thorndike, Wheeler, and Kennebec Large Print titles are designed for easy reading, and all our books are made to last. Other Thorndike Press Large Print books are available at your library, through selected bookstores, or directly from us.

For information about titles, please call:
(800) 223-1244

or visit our Web site at:

http://gale.cengage.com/thorndike

To share your comments, please write:

Publisher
Thorndike Press
10 Water St., Suite 310
Waterville, ME 04901